I lay waiting
between turf-face and demesne wall,
between heathery levels
and glass-toothed stone.

Seamus Heaney, *Bog Queen*

Our Numbered Bones

Katya Balen

CANONGATE

First published in Great Britain in 2026
by Canongate Books Ltd, 14 High Street, Edinburgh EH1 1TE

canongate.co.uk

1

Extract from 'Bog Queen' taken from *North* by
Seamus Heaney © The Estate of Seamus Heaney, 1975, 2025.
Reprinted by permission of Faber and Faber Ltd

British Library Cataloguing-in-Publication Data
A catalogue record for this book is available on
request from the British Library

ISBN 978 1 83726 510 7

Typeset in Bembo Std by Palimpsest Book Production Ltd,
Falkirk, Stirlingshire

Printed and bound by CPI Group (UK) Ltd, Croydon CR0 4YY

The manufacturer's authorised representative in the EU for product safety is
BGC Sustainability & Compliance, 7 avenue du Général Leclerc, Paris 75014
(gpsr@baldwinglobalconsulting.com)

For Patrick, of course

Our
Numbered
Bones

Also by Katya Balen

1

Yesterday I wandered the endless aisles in Surrey Quays Decathlon and I pretended to be someone else. I folded away the last few months and what I should have been doing and what I should have been buying. I focused on the bright bones of my knuckles as I gripped the trolley. I thought about what sort of person would buy walking gear. Someone who touches the tips of flowers and feels the softness of their petals. Someone who feels a connection to the whole world and marvels at the beauty of a snowflake. That person. I stood under the strip lighting and I closed my eyes and I tried to think about finding joy walking through a meadow or a wood or up a mountain. The hollow thump of basketballs skidding from a rack pulled me back to South London. I'd barely been able to imagine the shape of a tree.

I added thermal layers and waterproofs. They lay in the trolley like oily streaks. Shiny puddles. I couldn't afford them. I didn't even need them. But I wanted them. I wanted to shrug off the city and slip into someone else, someone far away. I added socks with gel padding and a coat that folds into your pocket and a plastic compass with a string for round your neck even though I didn't even know what it would mean if I was lost and knew which way was north. How does that even help? Someone better than me would know. I was already useless at stepping into this new life. I should have been better at make-believe.

I piled everything into my trolley and I bought the second cheapest walking boots because someone once told me you should never buy the cheapest. Just go one up. I think they might have been talking about wine. It didn't matter. It doesn't matter.

The total at the till was an electric shock. I fumbled for the right card and the woman asked if I was a hiker and I said yes because a lie is always easier now and it could become the truth. She added some glucose tablets for free and it made me cry and she looked like she wished she'd never said a word to me. She beeped the rest of the stuff through and kept her eyes on the red laser lines of her scanner. She was worried I was going to tell her everything. A stranger spilling her guts on the shiny wipe-clean floor. It's all right I wanted to say. I don't want to talk about it. I don't ever want to talk about it.

I stopped crying as soon as I got on the bus. London is too brittle and busy for that kind of thing. There was too much going on. Bags banging my ankles. Buggies jammed tight together in the wheelchair space. The city pressing against the windows. The hard shell of the bus hurtling me home for the last time in forever. My feelings back in their box.

Oh the box.

The box the box the box.

2

I leave today. My bag isn't packed. My train leaves in ninety minutes. The logic of timings and packing and planning escapes me. I am frozen. Staring at the ripples of waterproofs streaking the bed. I am sure I used to be able to do stuff like this. Get myself together. I am unravelling quietly. I don't want to make a fuss.

The cat jumps down from the top of the wardrobe. The thud of paws snaps me into something approximating action. Muscle memory. I fold up the strange slippery unfamiliar fabrics and I shove them into my wheely cabin bag and I wish I'd bought a holdall too. Who puts waterproof trousers into a bright red carry-on. It doesn't work. It doesn't fit together. There's not enough space after I've added all the walking stuff and I have to get JP's canvas shopping bags and stuff them with underwear and books and chargers and it's all a mess. Fine. I empty my bedside drawer of moisturisers and serums and eye creams because maybe this is the time to start using them. Escape to the country. Start a skincare regime. Fix it all with open fields and a really good night balm.

My fingers pause inside the drawer. I let them touch the

edge of the box. So small. But still somehow bigger than I'd thought it would be. Heavy. The weight of it all crushed to powder and ash and despair. Now pushed into the blackness. It's electric. I brush the wooden sides again. I think about pulling it towards me. Holding it in the palm of my hand. Feeling it heavy on my bones. Wrapping it in a scarf and slipping it into the suitcase. Taking it with me. Everywhere.

I can't.

Not now.

I pull my hand away.

Pick up a lip salve.

Close the drawer.

No more.

Lucy has sent me a message. A picture of a fox's penis. *Barbed! Bloody barbed! Patriarchy and biology are in cahoots.* This is the only way we really communicate now. Animal cocks and faux feminism. I send her an article about duck rape and sit on the edge of the bed and don't think about the box.

The box the box the box.

JP is trying to find the cat. His voice is stretching the vowels of the cat's name and every shout bounces through the flat and through my head. Now I can't think what else I need to pack. Outside there's the hiss of the double decker and the shouts from the burst of children just released from the school gates. The rumble of the train line and now the endless shouting for the cat who will be hiding under the sofa like always. Where else would he be? Why does it matter?

Seeeedneeeey. Seeeedneeeey.

There you are!

JP's voice is full of delight and wonder and the cat was under the sofa. For a second I think how it must be to live in a world where you can find genuine joy in an entirely predictable moment. Uncomplicated. Easy. Frictionless.

JP and I are very different people.

He is wonderful and sometimes that fact feels like a barb.

I try to wrap the handles of the canvas bags around the red case and they hang and twist. The whole thing becomes impossible to move. There are six flights of stairs between me and the ground floor. Greyslipped pavement stretching towards the Tube. Escalators. Corridors. Underground. I want to get into bed.

I've only just managed to get out of bed.

3

JP gives me his gym bag and a lift to the train station. He brushes his hand across the back of my neck and I flinch and pull away and his face pulls down. He takes a breath. He tells me he and Sidney will miss me. He's proud of me. This is a good step forward. The right thing to do. He'll make bouillabaisse when I'm back, with the proper fish from the fishmonger who gets it from Billingsgate, not just whatever Sainsbury's has vacuum-packed and yellow-stickered.

Sidney can have the heads he grins and I want to smile back at him. I want to be back where we were. He is trying. But I can't. I think of all those little headless rainbow bodies lying on our plastic worktops. Bones ripped from flesh. I swallow a mouthful of acid saliva.

JP I start but I can't shape the words and he doesn't want to hear them. He wants to tie us to a future together with fish stew and the bloody cat. I want to pull at the seams.

Anna. Don't.

His voice is a little boy's.

The sound sticks in my heart.

So I don't. I sew myself up instead.

I will go to her if you like JP says and I know he's rehearsed the words. He's too good and it's awful and I wish I'd never met him and that none of this had ever happened. It is hard to believe that everything was once so easy, so simple. Look at us now.

That's fine I say. *You don't need to. She wouldn't know. She won't know. It's a month. She's got that nice carer, activities. Puzzles. Zumba. Gymnastics. Nuclear fission.*

JP smiles uncertainly and I show my teeth to show it's a joke, it's all just a joke. It's just not funny.

And when you are back perhaps we can talk about what we do with— but I throw the door open before he can finish. Don't say it. He grabs my hand and I let him. I squeeze it so tightly I feel the dull grind of his tendons. I press it against my forehead as if my desperate mind will push my thoughts through our bones. I love you I think. I'm sorry. I'm so sorry.

And I get out of the car and I'm swallowed up by the mouth of the station and I try to leave it all behind and there are ghosts all around me.

4

The train empties out as it curls further and further away from the places people want to be. I read a book. I don't understand a word of it. It seems an impossible thing, to be able to create one of these. All those ideas. Fitted together on a page. Life happening in the right order. Moments constructed from fragments of feelings. Building towards something. How does anyone ever do it? It's ridiculous.

But I did it once. Just when things were starting to slip from my grasp and it was the only way to hold on. Such a long time ago. When all I had to worry about was a mother losing her mind.

There's a joke in there somewhere.

Even though I've got endless hours stretching out in front of me I don't write because I can't. I get my laptop out. Click the dart of the mouse around the screen. Check the news. Bad things happening everywhere. Then a bit of light relief. A parrot has been removed from display at a shop for swearing at customers. This is the kind of article they write to stop everyone losing their minds at the horror of it all. I sometimes wonder if these articles are a kind of government psy-op. Just enough whimsy to keep us from rioting. A dog got on a bus and went to a shopping centre all on its own. Oh that's so sweet, maybe no looting tonight.

I don't open a Word document. The train Wi-Fi stutters and cuts. I close the laptop lid. Leave it in front of me on the table like a slab of stone.

I cannot write. I am a cliché. First novel a quiet success. The imagined lives of J. Alfred Prufrock's women. Lines of poetry pulled into the shape of a whole new world. Applause in the broadsheets. Pensive profile headshots in the half light. An appetite for what might come next. Questions about my politics. My inspiration. My mind. What I eat for breakfast. Did I prefer *Game of Thrones* or *Succession*?

And now.

Nothing. Stuck. Blocked.

Empty.

And so here we are.

Another cliché. Running away from life to write my novel. My editor found the retreat for me when yet another deadline slipped by and I'd stopped lying about delivering the manuscript in a few weeks. She emailed the link and there was a line about understanding my difficult circumstances but she'd bolded the new delivery date. Her thoughts were with me. I didn't want to go. JP was furious with me. It was an anger I hadn't seen in him. I loved it. I tried to absorb every molecule of his emotions. Finally. He wasn't taking care of me. He wasn't trying to make things better. He was raising his voice. Throwing his arms out. Clenching his fists. Telling me to do something. Anything. Make a change. Stop this. Just stop this. I replied to my editor and thanked her for the opportunity. I'd love to go.

When it happened my editor sent flowers. Lilies. Funeral flowers. On the nose really, for someone who is supposed to work with nuance. And toxic to cats. JP put them on a high shelf in the living room. The smell wound its way through the whole flat. Thick. Bound up with death. It choked me. The water rotted to brown. JP threw them in the bin. A smear of pollen tattooed on his t-shirt.

I don't walk past the flower stall on the way to the Tube any more.

Even the air can catch you off balance.

The retreat is for struggling writers. It's a financial thing, they said when I asked what that word meant. You know, like you need to buy yourself the time. And if you need the space. Literal and metaphorical. The woman on the phone was a poet.

They gave me the cottage and a lump sum in my bank account on the condition that I thanked the organisation in the acknowledgements of my novel. As if the novel was a certainty. That it would definitely exist. I'd fallen for that trick before. There was a horror and a hope in it. But I just said *of course of course*. The money from my first tiny advance had been swallowed up by London and life and I felt suddenly giddily rich. I relied on JP too much. Now I had something of my own. This money will last, I told myself. What can you buy in the middle of nowhere. What can you do in the middle of nowhere except write. Look at the marvellous beauty of nature and write a book. That's it. That's all I have to do. Write a book.

The landscape changes. Of course it does. Houses peel away and the world is stripped bare. The sky is huge. A few trees pressed against the horizon. A twist of a hare, or is it a rabbit? I never did know the difference. Never needed to. Don't need to know now but it niggles. A problem I can solve. An easy answer. I get my phone out. No signal. Six messages from JP. Sent not long after I left. Photos of the cat. A love heart emoji. Telling me he misses me. That everything will be all right. Asking where the bin-bags are.

The train slows.

I watch the light spill into evening.

Here we are.

5

Just the soft dark now.

The earth shifts and recoils and changes around her.

It knots around her bones.

Feathers turn to ash and soil and she clings on.

Still solid.

Blind dark.

Old ache.

A map of roots twisting and talking to each other.

Bringing news of the air and the sky and the rain and all the things that were once so bright and beautiful.

But now

Now

There is

Something

new

6

I have to get a taxi from the station and the cost of it rattles me. There's an air freshener in the shape of a Christmas tree hanging from the rear-view mirror. New-car smell. The car is so old it has those patterned plush seats and the seatbelt buttons have faded to salmon pink. My father drove a car like this. Old but fit for purpose. I remember it parked outside our house. Layered thick with grime. He barely drove anyway. He liked to cycle to work. Trousers tucked into his socks. Yellow reflective sash. One of the best days of my life was when he dropped me at nursery. He usually left too early for that sort of thing. My mother was ill. He let me sit on the saddle as he wheeled it along the pavement. He pretended it was a horse, a unicorn, a royal carriage. We didn't tell my mother about our games. She didn't like me playing princesses. It wasn't feminist.

The scent of the air freshener clings to my throat. Catches in my lungs. I cough. The man offers me a wine gum. I take it. Hold it in my hand. It starts to stick and black my skin. The driver chats on about local pubs and his football team and he asks me what I'm doing in the cottage and if I'm another one of those writers. *Had that one in here a while back* he says. *You know. What's her name? The dragons one. She's done well, hasn't she. Films and everything. You going to have a film?* I shake my head no. His eyes meet mine in the mirror. I can feel pity rolling off him.

What sort of thing is it that you write then he says and I never know how to answer so I do an awkward laugh and jerk my shoulders up in a stiff show of embarrassment. Cough the air freshener from my chest. *Literary mainly. Women. I took the lives of some women from a poem. Gave them more than the poet had, I guess? But just stuff about life. Small. Quiet. Character studies I suppose. People and the everyday. Not much happens. Unsaid maybe.* I have to stop talking. The wine gum is disintegrating.

Right you are love. I've disappointed him. I suddenly want to give this stranger something with dragons and fire and ridiculous breathy sex in castle turrets.

He cranks the handbrake. *Far too clever for me I'm sure. Here you go. Mind yourself. They're always digging this place up. Bad enough even if they didn't. Too much water and mud. Can't keep itself stable. You got a torch?*

I don't have a torch. It's a stumbling bogsinking walk from the road to the cottage. I use my phone. The narrow whiteblue light slides uselessly over the ground. It catches on puddles. Shows me the reflection of the night sky. So many stars spread across the earth. For a moment they catch me. I stare up at this beautiful wonderful endless expanse of a whole universe sheltering over my head. Looking at lights that have already died and still shine on. I keep that thought in my chest. I walk on.

The house looms grey and low. It is an ancient building, put together roughly but properly. Solid stone walls and small windows. There is an attempt at a front garden. A wind-battered dry-stone wall winds from front to back in a wobbly loop. A path that is nothing more than slabs scattered in mud. Rustic. That's the word an estate agent would use. A bit of a mess.

The wheels of my suitcase twist and grip in the earth. JP's gym bag beats against my chest. The weight of it hanging in front of me is unbearable. Mud spits up my jeans. My breath is a milky ghost ahead of me but I am sweating by the time I get to the door. I am still holding the wine gum. The door has been left unlocked. The key hangs limply from the keyhole and I twist it free.

The cottage is small and cold. I step inside and I expect a cloak of heat but the temperature is like I am pulling the outside in around me. Someone has left a hall light on and it pushes the night back into the corners. I drop the bags on the floor. I have a moment of feeling utterly weightless and then my brain catches up with the trick. For a second the lightness was perfect. Air in my bones. Like I could just float away.

I keep my phone torch on until I find more light switches. I turn them all on. Click click click. Bright white floods. It doesn't suit the place. It needs those little lamps, pockets of warmth. Something that looks like candlelight. That's what it was built for. I once read that Danish students take lamps that cost a fortune with them to university. Hundreds of pounds' worth. Having a good lamp is part of their culture. Hygge. Cosiness. Soft fabric and pools of amber light and mid-century chairs. Our flat is sharp edges and flatpack. JP only cares about the kitchen. I don't care about anything. Not now.

One bedroom. Anonymous white sheets, chest of drawers, small desk, one bedside table. It makes the bed look lopsided. The curtains haven't been drawn and the night peers in. My own reflection startles in the cold glass. I pull the curtains across.

The bathroom has posh hand soap and those fluffy white towels you get in hotels. Rolled up tight and rested carefully on a three-legged stool. There's a bath but no separate shower. Just a flimsy hose hooked halfway up the wall over the tub and the kind of plastic curtain that adheres instantly to wet skin. I suppose I've got time for endless baths. Slipping into hot water. Scrubbing off the bog and the mud. Staring at the ceiling. Having literary thoughts.

The sink is cracked. Spidery edges traced with grey. I stare at the lines too long. Blink to break the spell.

The living room has beams and a bookcase and a wood-burning stove. The kind we're not supposed to have. Filling the sky with more pollutants than a 4x4 or a Boeing 737 or something. Choking our trees and our children. Killing off the world with every cosy winter evening. Or maybe they're all right now. I can't keep up. I can't make the space to worry about it.

Fire tools. A poker. Dustpan and brush. A wicker basket

stuffed with logs. A few woodlice crawling along the veins of the bark. Ash scattered on the hearth. Soft and feathered.

I turn away.

Enough.

In the kitchen I find a note on the scrubbed wooden table along with a bottle of red wine and a packet of biscuits. My stomach squeezes. I didn't think about food. I hardly ever do now. I try to remember if I saw anywhere to buy food on the taxi ride. No. Hard to tell though. No streetlamps. Just the car headlights fighting the night. It doesn't matter anyway.

I check my phone. No signal. No Wi-Fi. That's the whole point. Just you and your endless endless thoughts that somehow need to be shaped into a book. Running so far away that your problems can't follow you. No thinking about what happened. No contact with JP. No contact with my mother. Try to pull the barbed hook from my cheek. Snap the line.

I went to see my mother just before I left. I hadn't been in so long. Too long. I felt the guiltpinch of it under my skin. I caught the bus to the care home and I walked across the grey choke of the ring road and through the dim corridors that smelled like piss and school dinners and I found her sitting in a chair and staring into nothing.

Her edges had frayed even further. She was blending into the air. I told her I was sorry. I held the hand that once held mine. The bones were sharp. I could see the trace of life under her skin. A network of blue. I told her

I'd been very busy and I could feel the lie black on my tongue. She pulled her hand away. She looped imaginary threads around her fingers. She knitted the air and flickered and flapped and her hands hummed like a restless bird. She didn't know how long it had been. She didn't know that time was split in two now.

I wondered what time is like for her. A circle or a line or something else. Something cloudy and nebulous and hard to keep hold of.

She had forgotten me. There was a moment when my childhood seemed to concertina in front of me. My mother and father each holding one of my hands and swinging me over puddles. One two three wheeeeee. My mother dropping me off in the playground for my first day of school. Telling me to come home with three new things I'd learned. Story time with all of us curled up in bed. My father's side of the bed suddenly cold and empty one day. My mother hanging Christmas lights around my room when I found the dark too much to bear. My mother dropping me off at university and leaving five twenty-pound notes hidden in my sock drawer. There would never again be moments like these.

It was a horror and a relief. It could have been different. If I had been better. If I had visited more. Maybe I could have held her together. Maybe her eyes wouldn't have slid past mine and stared out at the low milk-tea sky. Maybe she would have found some words inside her picked-clean brain. Maybe she would have been able to do what mothers are supposed to do. Maybe she would have been able to hold me and tell me everything is going to be all right.

It feels like my fault that I have lost her.

But she's the lucky one. I am so jealous of her fluttering mind that I feel sick. I grind my teeth until they squeak. I want to melt into another world. I want to pluck the memories from my brain like the feathers from a bird. I want to lie in a bed and watch dust motes dance and never have to remember.

7

I shake away the thoughts of my mother and I sit down to read the note. The nearest shop is an hour's walk and the hot water is on a timer. The walks are lovely round here. There's an OS map on the bookshelves. Someone will come in once a week to clean. Bins are Tuesdays. Drag them half a mile up onto the road. Hope you brought walking boots! Good luck with your writing. Remember us in your acknowledgements!

It is piercingly cold. It is fighting its way into my bones. I should light the fire. Burn some life back into me. I get up and kneel by the dusty hearth. Scrabble through the basket for kindling and paper.

I can't light a fire. Obviously. I have lived in a flat in a new-build block for far too many years. I remember my mother doing it. Making light work of it. Tasks with her hands suited her. She never understood why I wanted to bother with books and a brain. She said it wouldn't make me happy. Ha.

I wonder what thoughts she has lost. I never knew them to start with. I never thought to ask.

I build a pyramid of logs and add a handful of wood

scraps. I throw in a firelighter and two scrunched pages of the *Guardian*. The flames burst bright. Ash clouds the grate. I rock back. Everything can be turned by fire. Reduced by flames. All the stuff of life. Shrunk down to grey and grit and powder and black. All made the same. I can't decide if that's some sort of universal justice or the most terrible thing in the world.

When I was a child I once searched along the banks of the Thames for treasure. I'd seen it on TV. People finding gold coins and secrets from the past. I thought I'd be rich. I'd be on TV too. Showing off my hoard and talking about luck and chance and skill. I really thought it would come true. I think it's one of the only things I can remember believing in. I clung to the idea.

My mother waited with her patience fraying and unravelling on the stones. I couldn't believe she'd taken me at all. Every second was frantic in case she changed her mind. I picked up rocks and lumps of twisted plastic. Bricks and curves of iron. I wanted gold or jewels or magic bottles with genies hammering on the glass. My fingers were slick with the city mud. Clay under my fingernails. Streaks of it on my trousers. My mother reaching for the wet burn-and-rub of a face wipe.

I found the jawbone glinting bright in the watery sun. Turned yellow with time and tide. Just the lower jutting curve. Piratical. Teeth still anchored and rooted. I picked it up and held the lightness of it. I showed it to my mother and she shrank back.

What is it I said. *What's it from?* Flesh and fur stripped away. The mask slipped from the skull. I couldn't tell. I counted the teeth instead. Fourteen. I liked holding something that made my mother smaller.

Sheep she said grimly and I nodded. It's only now that I wonder how she knew. Or maybe she didn't. She plucked an animal from the air and I believed her. I took the jawbone home and kept it in a jar. It grew mould. Green and black. The sides of the jar clouded. My mother wouldn't keep it any longer. She untwisted the lid and threw it on the fire. I sat and wrote a poem and said a prayer I'd heard at school and she rolled her eyes. I threw the poem into the flames and burned my words. But the bones wouldn't burn. They blackened and splintered. We swept teeth from the grate. Shards and molars tipped into the bin instead. My mother said the fire needed to be hotter.

I try not to think about that heat. The fury of it. What it does. The box.

The box the box the box the box the box.

I crumble a biscuit between my fingers but I don't eat it. I can't bring myself to eat it. I brush the crumbs into the huge white mouth of the Belfast sink and rinse them away immediately. I unpack. Fold and sort. Drawers neat and full. Toothbrush in the mug by the sink. Serums lined up on a shelf by the mirror. Neater than in the flat. All in order. Exactly like I live here now. A new person. Ordered. I use the bathroom. I wash my face. Scrub away the journey. See new lines that are spidering at the corners of my eyes.

Cracking up. I get into the pyjamas that still smell like my old life and then I get into the sleepworn sheets of the creaking bed and I sleep and I sleep and I sleep.

8

I dream of her. She is dead. Like always. Not pale like you'd expect. Dusky. Dark. Angry at it all. Like nothing could make her more furious than death. The unfairness of it. The rage purpling her skin. Turning her eyes blood dark.

Silence. A creaking of bones. A settling into the horror.

Then there is a rush of air into stiffening lungs and she is alive and there is nothing but pure joy for a single heartbeat.

She is screaming. I don't care. It's golden. It's music. It's life. Then it twists. The pitch changes. Sharper. Stranger. Animal. Monster. I try to make it stop. Make it change back. Nothing works. I am not helping her. I can't help her.

Her skin is pale now. The fury is draining. Fading away. Turning to porcelain and glass. Fragile. Fearful. Grey spider-web cracks fluttering and spreading. Splitting her apart.

The walls are melting. She is melting. She is sinking down. I can't hold on to her. I watch her slide like candlewax through the cracks in the floor. I just watch. I wait. I wait until every single slippery scrap of skin has disappeared and then I mop and mop and mop.

I mop and I scrub and I bleach and I try to remove the stains and my eyes burn.

9

I wake up and the dream swirls away from me. Sweat in my eyes. Heart wild. Deep breaths. The horror and the hope. I am still drugged by it. I don't want to keep it.

Try to forget.

I'm here to forget.

I get up into the freezing air of the cottage. I keep the duvet wrapped round my shoulders. The thermostat on the wall is one of those old ones that clicks when I spin its wheel to 22. 23. 24. 25. I am always cold. I can't keep the heat inside my bones. The radiators don't wheeze and clank into life. I remember the note. The timer. I shiver.

I have slept longer than I usually do and the morning is high and bright. The world stretches on and on outside the windows. Flat. The horizon stitching sky to earth. The lack of anything but the land. There is no one. Not a single home or heartbeat. It feels like I am at the very edge of something. Just keep walking and you'll reach the end. Tumble into nothing. That sounds nice.

I find a bag of ground coffee next to the kettle. I make some and try to note down every syllable of what I'm doing. Notice the texture of the grounds as I heap them into the cafetière. The touch of the kettle. The slip of steam on my skin as it boils. Little jigsaw pieces of life. Build a scene. Write it down. There you go. A book.

I sip the coffee slowly but it burns my mouth anyway. I push my tongue into the side of my raw cheek. Not too bad. I could write a line about it. Right now. Just scribble down a few fragments of the pain in a notebook. Turn it into something meaningful later. I don't.

I pull the map down from the bookshelves but the squares don't make sense to me. I push my fingers into my eyeballs until stars start to burst behind my eyelids. I try again and then I leave it on the coffee table. Another day maybe. The rest of the shelves are full of books by all the other authors who have stayed here. I see the dragon one. Fat. Hundreds and hundreds of pages. Hundreds of thousands of words. CGI fire and dragon scales scattered down its well-cracked spine. I pull it down. Look at the spikey faux-medieval font and the runic patterns stamped on the front. I put it back. The other books are slimmer. More modest. Prize-winning though. A quiet confidence in their plain covers and cryptic titles. I don't take any of them down. Their spines are unbroken.

There's a glass bottle of cow's milk in the fridge and a dusty bag of porridge and a few jars of pasta sauce in one cupboard. I open another. Salt. Pepper. Pre-ground in white plastic tubs. Cooking oil. It looks cloudy and the bottle is filmy with grease. No spices. Two crumbling stock cubes. I don't care about pre-ground pepper or jarred sauces or shop-bought stock but JP would have a heart attack. When he brought me home from the hospital he made nothing but soups for days. Homemade stock because the stuff you buy in the supermarket is just palm oil and sugar and salt. Terrible. Processed. Delicious. He went to the overpriced farmers' market and came back with bags and bags of raw animal flesh. I couldn't look at it. I didn't know how he could bear it. I went to bed. He sliced and crushed and stripped and cleaved. Did you know the word cleave has two opposite meanings? To stick together. To pull apart. A contranym. I used to find things like that interesting.

JP worked for hours and hours. Boiling up bones. The walls were streaming with the sweat of it all. I wouldn't eat a mouthful and he didn't know what to do. This was all he could do.

I didn't get out of bed for seven weeks and five days.

My bones made sharp shapes against my skin.

10

The earth is charged and she

is coming

apart

from it

all

11

I close the cupboards.

Maybe what I need now is food. Something wholesome. Fill up the cupboards and hunker down. Light the fire. Use a fountain pen and one of those notebooks with the leather covers. Each sentence exquisite and expensive. Make a cosy nest and just write and write and write.

I empty one of JP's canvas shopping bags. He has a thousand. He has too much stuff. He collects it all. Surrounds himself with scraps and pieces. Filling the void. He will not let any of it go. He is not a hoarder. Not one of those people who can fill a house with towers of newspapers. Bathtub stuffed with copies of the *Radio Times* dating back to 1982. But he has trouble letting go. I would burn it all.

JP is a goldfish. If you put a goldfish in a tiny tank, it will stay small. If you give it a huge aquarium it will grow. JP expands to fill the space he is given. I have not given him enough.

The bag is empty. Wires and underwear and scraps of paper and a notebook and a handful of pens. Leave the mess on the bed. Don't think about the bag filled with marbled slabs of flesh wrapped in greased paper. The smell of blood. Metal and death.

I get dressed for the walk. Base layers. Leggings under my jeans. Shiny jacket. Take the tags out first. Thick socks. Whole new skin. Itchy. Compass in my pocket. If I end up lost and found by some locals then at least I can pretend I knew what I was doing. That I know what I'm doing.

I lace up my walking boots and go. Alone into the flat earth.

12

The shop has a huge plate glass window. The sort that should let the light stream in. The sort that makes the landscape feel closer. Pressing through the glass. The sort of windows that in London would mean an artisan bakery or a café fitted out entirely in plywood. Nine pounds for a small pastry and an oat flat white. This window is grimy with bog salt and so cluttered with notices and missing cat posters and signs that no one can see out and the light can't get in.

I am sweating from the walk. I feel embarrassed. My legs whirring like a beetle. Chest shrieking. Shifting air through straw-tight lungs. Just an hour on the flat winding road. I didn't see a single car and if there had been the offer of a lift I would have climbed in without a second's thought for all of the dead girls littering history. I would have been glad to join them. The thought should shock me but it doesn't. They never do now.

Inside there is too much stuff and too little space. Racks and shelves rammed. I feel squeezed. I walk past the metal frames loaded with yellow Calor gas bottles and plastic bottles of Castrol. Windscreen wash glowing alien blue. Orange nets of kindling and sacks of cheap dog food. Picture of a shiny Labrador panting its head off on the packet. JP buys Sidney's food from some sort of organic company who don't use artificial additives or ash or grains or some shit. It costs a fortune. It comes with Sidney's name printed on the box and uses the same graphic designer as overpriced breweries. It is absurd. JP loves that cat so much. He is supposed to be our shared pet but he doesn't like me. That's fine. He's free to choose. I would choose not to spend ninety quid a month on feeding the ungrateful bastard but it's not my decision to make. We got him together. We went to a rescue centre near our flat. The woman was mad. She was suspicious of anyone who wanted to rehome a cat and that meant that she was suspicious of literally everyone she ever met. It must have been exhausting. She asked us if we had criminal records. She asked us if we would ever leave the cat on its own. She asked us if we had a garden. She asked us if cars went past our house. *We live in London* I said helplessly. *Surely everyone who comes here does?* She pressed her mouth into a flat line. We had failed. We were not allowed one of her cats. We got Sidney from a litter down the road. Two hundred and fifty pounds for a black and white moggy.

I pick up a basket and weave through the aisles. Everything is neon-wrapped and shelf-stable. I buy dried pasta and Pot Noodles and oven chips and cheese in a tube. The kind that claims to have prawns pasted through it. I add biscuits and multipacks of chocolate bars. All the stuff that JP hates. Plastic food. Perfect. Everything as fake as possible, please. Ultra-processed is the new carb is the new fat is the new sugar. I add a bottle of Coke and take the lid off before I've paid. I drink the whole thing. Sugar snaps at my blood. I feel better. More awake. The caffeine sparks. My lungs loosen.

A small girl watches me. Big eyes with those impossible lashes that mascara could never achieve. Hair spiked up into one of those little pineapples on top of her head. Jumper all covered in unicorns and rainbows. Glitter and pink. Ridiculously small shoes. The kind that light up purple as she backs away from me. Reaches for her mother's hand. Fingers sliding together. Perfect tessellation. I look away. Pick up another bottle of Coke.

I pay and I get a little thrill at spending the money meant for literature and art and greatness on chocolate Hobnobs. I feel like I'm cheating at a game that I didn't even want to play. The woman at the register looks at my canvas bags. Her eyebrow twitches.

Looks like a good night in love she says as she scans another packet of crisps. Nice 'n' Spicy Nik Naks. I do not meet her eye. Just a brief nod. I cannot be bothered to engage. I stare at the pictures of metastatic lung cancer behind her and wonder how long it would take if I started smoking. I buy twenty Marlboro Reds and a lighter.

The canvas bags were the wrong choice. Obviously. They slide off my shoulders and bite into my palms. I have to keep stopping. Bowed by the weight of food I don't even want. Won't even eat.

One foot in front of the other. A slow trudge back until the cottage lifts itself grey out of the gloom.

To work.

13

I try to light the fire again. It fails again. Of course. I leave it smoking its way to nothing and I make a Pot Noodle. Put it in a bowl. I'm not an animal. Make another coffee. Sit at the little desk in the living room. Laptop screen buzzing white and waiting. Notebook open. Pens laid out. Highlighters and everything. You never know.

A few lines. Break the horror of the blank page. Delete them. Circle back to the first sentence. Type it again. Change the font. And again. Get the line spacing just right. 1.5? 2? Justify the text. Delete it all.

The only story tapping its way in my brain is the one I never want to tell. The words of it are chattering in their chains.

Shut up shut up shut up.

I need air. I need to get out. I can't sit here cramped up at this desk with nothing but my own thoughts.

I'll go out. Walk across the flatlands. Find a story in nature or something. That's why I'm here. Not to coop myself up in a cottage and stare at a screen. To get out and see a new angle of the old world. Let the grass inspire me. The sky. The mud.

I put the walking boots back on. Dirt clings to their soles. Falls off in fat clods as I walk.

Step into the endless land.

Out.

14

The cold hits me in the chest. The wind is sharp. Nothing for it to catch on until it finds me. Sliding over the flats and fens and bogs. Relentless. My ears ring and my skin burns. It feels good. Ice and fire. Can't think about anything but the knife sliding right through me.

I didn't bring the map. I'll just walk. Walk and walk and walk and find my own way. That's how it should be. Step off the path. Find something unexpected. Put it in a novel. Get back on the path.

I think about what would happen if I got lost. If I twisted an ankle on a hidden tree root and couldn't crawl for help. If I slipped into a ditch and the dank water bubbled down my throat. If I had a heart attack out in the wide empty open. If I was pulled under into the bogs below and bound tight to the earth. If there was a lone madman with a machete and a hatred of women lurking somewhere in the beyond.

I find each death a comfort.

In the first few weeks I told JP all the ways I'd like to die. It was the most I'd spoken since it happened. I'd just been buried in bed. A shape pressed flat by blankets and grief. Motionless. My voice was cracked. Dry. My throat clicked with the effort of it. I didn't cry. I just made a list. Calm and clear. Fire. Drowning. Pills. Stabbing. Splitting the skin of my wrists. The right way. Down. Not across. Everybody knows that now. Hit by a bus. Plane crash. Car crash. Train crash. Falling from an open window. Tumbling off a high rise. Choking. Cardiac arrest. Sudden-onset peanut allergy. Blood clot the size of a fist. Brain aneurysm. Nothing too quick though. I'd want to know it was happening. Feel the relief.

JP locked up all the knives and tablets and windows. But I was just talking. That's the thing. I couldn't do any of it. I wanted it to happen *to* me. Just passive and willing and waiting. Being pulled under the salt-sharp waves and my lungs filling with brine and my blacked-out brain fading fast. Feeling the plummet of a plane and sitting back against the headrest and closing my eyes while everybody else screams. The first thump of metal as the bus shatters my bones and keeps on going. Watching the quicksilver slice of a knife pull apart my skin. The firework burst of blood behind my eyes. Seeing the first flicks of flame tonguing their way under the bedroom door and thinking oh yes there it is. There it is. This is it. Finally. I've been waiting for you. Thank you. Let's go.

But he didn't get it. He told me to stop. Thumped his knuckles against the wall. He left a smudge on the paintwork. I'd never seen him make a fist before. He told me I was scaring him. That I had to stop this. He asked me how

I'd feel if he did this to me. So I stopped talking about it. I stopped talking about all of it.

Death was just something I liked to play with.

15

As if

     that would ever be

the end

of it

     all

16

The landscape is all the same. Just green–gold grass spikes and brown mud and sudden pools of fetid water. It is strange. It might be beautiful. It doesn't feel like it is part of time. Like it has always been this way and will always be this way. Just frozen. Stuck. Still. Never changing, no matter the whirl of chaos and pain around it.

My feet are sucked into the ground and the mud grips. I remember being scared of the idea of quicksand as a child. Of being pulled under with no warning. I wonder if the same happens here. Another quiet way to die. Stuck. Letting the world carry on above you.

I think the note in the cottage would have said something if there were quicksand.

The boots have rubbed blisters into my heels. I sit on the soft ground and pull them off. I sink a little into the earth. The laces bite my fingers. Socks off too. Raw circles patterning my skin. The smell of iron and flesh. Skin peeling off in petals. Melting away. My stomach turns. Too familiar. I put my socks back on and my nails catch the blisters and I let the pain push the memory away.

Maybe I'll get trench foot. Does that even kill you?

Something else to google later. Just slowly rotting from the toes up. I'd let it spread and poison me. Turn my heart black. My blood to sludge.

The cold plunges into my bones. I chatter my teeth. Remember the grinning half-moon of sheep jaw. The fire.

I check my phone but there's still no signal. I've been outside for seventeen minutes. I am cold and wet. The world isn't beautiful. I see nothing but endless grass and the same sky reflected in dark water. I can't think how to sketch the shape of the clouds with words.

I am not connecting with nature. I haven't found joy in a leaf. I haven't thought of the perfect way to describe a cloud. I haven't stumbled across my novel. Of course I haven't. I am stuck. Still.

I am failing. I want to go home. But not that home. Home to the past. I am so stupid that it burns. But not hot enough.

The water has soaked into my trousers. The seat. All along where my legs have touched the ground. I didn't bother with the waterproof ones. They were a step too far. Something for fishermen and women with a minimum of three spaniels. The stain spreads dark and silty across the denim. Tide marks of the bog. It stinks. Mud and sulphur and something darker. Deeper. Rotten. Like the ground is churning its guts up through the soil. I put my hands into the ice dark of it. It is so cold I can't feel it at all. Like pulling silk through my fingers. My nails are rimmed with dirt. Silt in the lifelines that cross my palms. I twirl the water like I am a child. Watch it catch and drop. Beads of it turning from sky to earth as they fall. I imagine I can feel the heartbeat of the land. The drum and pulse of life underneath. I can put my hand through the ground and feel the underworld. The soft dark of another place. Something hidden and beautiful.

I can feel it.

The life below.

I am going mad.

I tie my laces.

I walk.

17

The water cannot carry her

       The earth cannot hold her

The roots recoil and the sky is splitting

     Everything

in two

And then there is sunlight

 And her heart cannot beat faster and her stoneheavy
  tongue cannot shape a scream

 And her fingernails cannot claw at the broken ground
  and the spilled light

     But the ground feels her pain and the
       earth spits again

And there we are

       Here we are

   now

18

The voices come from the direction of the pale sun. The bark of a dog. The shout. *Leave it Tam leave it for god's sake.* Carried over the flats. Like they're standing next to me. Two men.

I walk towards the sound. See the sudden streaks of the people against the horizon. Bent over. Hands over mouths. A man holding the collar of a dog. A collie. Black and white and lithe. Proper country dog. Bottle-brush tail sweeping and misting the air with mud. One of the men crouches down. I see his hand stretch out. Pull back in a lightning crack of disgust.

God is it it's bloody isn't it oh bloody hell have you got signal stupid question get back to the Landy and we'll sort it I'll have to stay here take the dog bloody hell Tam just go with him no I haven't got a lead he doesn't need one well carry him or something then he can't stay here can he oh for god's sake just go will you

I am pulled forward. Magnetic. Driven towards whatever this horror is. It's not something I could ever control. Rubber-necking. Twisted and turned by some unseen force, dragged towards tragedy. I have always done it. One of my very first memories is running towards a child in the playground. Her knee bright and bloody. A shock of white beneath a flap of skin. Gravel tattooing her shins. Too stunned to even scream. I crouched down and I held her hand and all the teachers told me I was kind. I just wanted to be part of it all. I wanted to see what was beneath our skin.

I have only ever seen one car crash. JP was driving. We were stuck in endless tailbacks. Hours and hours of sitting on the dusty motorway. My bladder bruised and aching. Desperate. Sharing a crushed Twix, one finger each. JP trying to make me have both. Me resisting even though I definitely wanted two. The children in the car next to us pressing their noses into the windows and flattening their strawberry tongues against the glass. I gave them a little wave and pulled a funny face and they ducked down out of view. Finally we were funnelled down one lane. High-vis police officers ushering us on and a wave of gratitude at the delicious movement of the car made me wind down the window and say *thank you thank you for everything you do*. The kind of thing I'd laugh at JP for saying. The kind of thing I'd never normally say. Never normally think. JP kept his eyes straight ahead. *Don't look* he said as we inched past the flap of the plastic tape and the bright blue wash of ambulance lights. *Trust me just don't look. This kind of thing stays with you forever. You can't unsee it. Just look at the number plate in front. Keep your eyes fixed on that, chérie. Add up the numbers. Make a poem from the letters. Don't turn your head. Listen to my voice. Just don't look.*

Of course I looked. I had to look. I was inches from life and death and disaster and I wanted to know about it. There was blood on the road. Black as oil. *Dark blood is bad isn't it* I said to JP. *Something about it being from deeper inside you.* Someone's boot was standing upright in the blood. One of those leather ones that motorcyclists wear when they take their safety seriously enough to gear up properly but not seriously enough not to ride a motorbike. Thick dinosaur ridges and a wedged sole. Like an alien carapace shed in the middle of the M3. *How did that end up there* I started and JP just stared straight ahead. Knuckles white. A stupid question. I saw the crumple of a car. A figure wrapped in a silver blanket. I could see how the light bounced as she trembled. I could imagine the words spilling from her.

He came out of nowhere.

He was going so fast.

I just didn't see him.

I didn't mean for it to happen.

Twenty metres from that one boot was a body. Twisted like a twig. The lower leg of his leathers flat and empty. Everything about him all wrong. A strange stillness. I'd never seen a body before but there was something animal and instinctive in my knowledge of death. The man was dead. I would have bet my life on it.

JP was right. The body stayed painted behind my eyes. I would sometimes take out the memory and examine it. Try to push meaning into it. Try to think about being that close to death and how it made me feel. I didn't mind it. It wasn't connected to me. It was a tragedy. But it wasn't mine. I was all right with it.

At the hospital JP couldn't stop staring. He held death tight to his chest.

I wish I hadn't looked. I should have kept my eyes straight ahead.

That kind of thing stays with you forever.

You can't unsee it.

I walk forward.

19

The sky has not changed
and there is something beautiful and
terrible in the truth of that

20

The man looks up as I approach. His face is a mask. Skin pulled waxy over flesh. Cheeks threaded with the kind of veins only wind and whisky can produce. He is wearing a tweed flat cap and a Barbour jacket and the kind of wellies that they only sell outside the M25.

God careful where you step he says and puts his hands up to those scribbled cheeks. I look down but there is nothing beneath my boots except the sink of silt and mud. I look back at him, waiting. If you leave a silence long enough people will fill it. Usually I wish they wouldn't.

He doesn't speak. He looks sickened. His skin is turning grey. He just points to the ground at his own feet. I follow his clubbed finger.

It takes a moment for me to make sense of the earth. It's like a magic eye puzzle. You stare and stare and suddenly there it is.

It's been there all along.

Just waiting.

A face in the earth.

A statue I say stupidly. Why has someone buried a statue. A student prank. A game. Out here in the salted bogs.

Nothing else to do I suppose. Drinking and wandering the world. Is there a university anywhere near here? I think there is. There must be. Or an agricultural college or something. My brain is running on, spooling out thoughts faster than I can catch them.

The man shifts.

Police will be here soon he says. He has the sort of voice that is all marbles in the mouth. He forces his tongue around the words. *Then we'll know. Hope so. Hope that's what it is. But round here . . . wouldn't be the first. You know?*

I don't know. I am not listening to him any more. I can't help it. His words fade off into the beige sky and I am staring down. I can't look away. I can't turn my head. The air crackles. That magnet pull. There is a line between us. I follow it.

The face looks as if it is carved from pewter. The skin is dark. Leathered. Like it has absorbed the earth around it and let it bleed through to the surface. I can see lines spidering at the corners of its closed eyes. A mouth with a rosebud curve. A nose made flat and twisted by the turn of the earth. I need to see more. I need to be closer. I kneel down and the man makes a noise in his throat but I don't look up.

I stare at the face pushing itself up through the mud and into the empty air and the edges of the world fall away and for seconds or minutes or hours it is just us and we stare at each other and we follow the lines of our broken faces and we feel the charge that runs between us and the earth grips us both tight.

51

And there is something lightning sharp inside me and the words sear bright hot into my brain.

I know you.

21

She knows

She knows

She knows

22

I want to stroke her cheek. I want to cradle her face in my hands. I want to press my forehead to hers and feel the cool crack of her skin on mine. I want to read her thoughts with my palms. When I reach my fingertips out towards her the man calls out and his voice is a panic whipped on the wind and it is enough to stop me. My fingers trace the air.

You can't touch it he says sharply and I feel a stab of something like fury. *It.* But I am being strange and I don't know why. I recoil. Hold my hands up in surrender.

The police he says again and he's softened his voice. Perhaps he thinks I am mad. That he must be kind to people like me. *It's just the police. They won't like it.* He is looking at me from the sides of his eyes. He puts his hands into the pockets of his Barbour and puffs out his breath.

The police arrive. Stamping over the soil with their big boots and their huge yellow jackets. A Land Rover with its blue lights cold and still rumbles behind them. They stand around and talk into their radios and rub their hands together. They talk to the man and then to me and when they find out where I'm staying they ask if I'm writing about dragons too.

They take a statement from me. I don't have very much to say. I don't tell them I nearly cupped her face in my hands. I don't know if the man did. I tell them I thought she was a statue. I tell them she looks like she's waiting for something. They look at me strangely.

I want them to leave.

My mouth tastes bitter.

But more and more arrive and they zip into those papery white onesies and pad around and start to scrape and poke and photograph. The white-hot flash of the camera repeats in front of my eyes even when they stop and I press my fingers into my skull to try to make it fade.

You can get on love, go and take a paracetamol or something for that head says one of the officers who earlier wanted to know if I at least had a TV deal. *It's freezing out here. Go and have a hot bath and a nice cup of tea. Forget about all of this stuff. You don't need to worry about any of it.*

I will worry about all of it. The police are moving on from me now. Fiddling with tape. Pressing buttons on their radios. Arguing about who has to walk back to the Land Rover for a piece of equipment. I am dismissed.

I don't want to leave her.

I walk back to the cottage. Every step tugs. An invisible rope. Fraying and taut.

23

I sleep badly. I get up and don't bother with a shower. I put on soft tracksuit bottoms and a hoody. I make a breakfast that I do not eat. I think about her. I brush my teeth and spit frothed to blood-streaked white into the sink. I am falling apart. I sometimes have that dream where my teeth fall out. My friend Lucy told me once that those dreams happen when you are afraid of dealing with something. Ha. I had them all the time when I was very small. What was I afraid of then, I wonder. I woke up crying once, running my tongue around my nearly brand-new mouth. All present and correct. My father came in. His hair rumpled from sleep. Sticking up like a chicken's feathers. It made me laugh. He made me laugh. Always. I told him about my dream and he held me on his lap. I remember his smell more than his face. Musk and cotton and beard and earth. *That's just the tooth fairy* he said. *She sends those dreams to say hello. It means that one day soon she'll come to visit for real. She'll bring you a whole gold coin. Isn't that something? Isn't that wonderful?* I asked why she wanted my teeth. *She builds a palace from them, Anna. A beautiful palace that shines like a pearl.* I thought it was disgusting. He said I was right, it was a bit weird. *But a gold coin isn't a bad exchange, and you don't have to live there.* I never spent that first pound when it came a few months later. It was too special. Too inextricably linked with that sleepy night-time cuddle. That fairy story. That treacle-soft safety and happiness. It was so easy back then.

I do not write. Of course. I do try. I sit and stare at a blank Word page for an hour. Maybe two. Time bends. I am thinking only of her. My coffee steams and goes cold.

I cannot stand this.

I must go back to her.

I get dressed. Properly this time. The right layers. I step into the frigid air. I retrace my steps from yesterday. It takes me over an hour. I get turned around. Time isn't right. It can't be. It won't follow a straight line. The sun is high. How can that be?

I find her eventually. The plastic flutter of police tape rattling in the breeze. The activity from yesterday has melted away. Just a single police officer. Cold and still. Standing guard. Bored. I recognise him from yesterday. The same guy who told me there was nothing more I could offer them. That I should take myself home.

I approach and he eyes me. He recognises me after a second.

Back again he asks and he smiles a sweet smile. He is young. *You don't look like a grave robber.*

What's happening with her I ask. I do not bother with pleasantries. He raises an eyebrow.

Her?

I stop.

I know. I just know. I cannot explain it. I do not explain it. I just wait. The air is ice. I shiver. I crane my neck. I want to see her. There is a tent erected over her.

Above my pay grade he says. *I am told to stand here. So here I stand. That's as much as I can tell you.*

Can I see her I ask. *Please.*

He blinks. He wasn't expecting that. He begins to shake his head.

I'm a writer I say before he can tell me no. It feels like I am lying. But he stops. Sometimes it is enough to bend the rules. To impress people. I press my advantage. *I'm a writer. Just research. I won't touch her. I won't touch anything. I just want to see her.*

I shouldn't he says and I know he will.

He does.

He parts the mouth of the blue tent. He will not let me inside. He lets me stand in the doorway. I can see her.

There she is.

She takes my breath away.

The rope tugs.

I stay stock-still. I stare. I take in what I couldn't yesterday. The lines and angles of her. The shadow and light of her. The hardness and the soft. She is extraordinary. I know her. I feel my fingers reaching out. I want to cup the curve of her face.

The police officer clears his throat. I jump and pull my

hand back. I do not know how much time has passed. I realise I am very cold.

Probably best if you get off he says. *Got some others coming up. You're not meant to be here, you know.*

Will I find out I say and my teeth clash together with the cold. *Will I find out what's happening? What's happened?*

Round here? says the officer and he laughs. He takes off his peaked cap. His hair is surprisingly beautiful. Auburn curls. The kind you see on cherubs and toddlers. *The pub will probably find out before we do.*

24

I walk to the pub. I cannot take these thoughts back to the cottage with me. I cannot sit alone squeezed by the stone walls. I am rattled. Literally. I am trembling. My muscles spasm. My teeth chatter. My bones knock together. I run my tongue around my mouth. My cheeks taste earthy and metallic. I can see the body. The face. The knowledge of it. Haunting me.

I follow the road back towards the station. The pub is somewhere there. Near the shop. I saw it hulking low and square this afternoon. Swinging sign. The Black Bull or the White Horse or something as unmemorable. Traditional ales and fish and chips. Chips are a good idea maybe. Listen to the locals talk.

The sky is clouded. Flattening itself over the land. Curling itself under the edges of the horizon. I feel pressed between the two spaces. I want to walk back to where I've just been. There is that magnet pulling me back to the earth. I want to be there with her.

It is like falling in love. Seeing her. That is the only way to describe it. JP once told me that the moment he saw me he was in love. I laughed. I was delighted. I was fun back then. I had always had the knack of finding something happening in a tiny secret corner of the city. I would take him by the hand on a Saturday morning and drag him to an unspoiled flea market. The kind where the finds are good and a reasonable price. No tourists or tat. I bought a mid-century lamp in bright orange for a fiver. JP found a box of vintage martini glasses that were perfect for the restaurant's bar. I haggled the seller down to ten quid. It was one of the proudest moments of my life. The next week we went to a rave in a church. A pop-up Korean restaurant in an old lady's living room. *You open up the world for me* JP said and I cuffed him lightly round the head for being so saccharine and so unBritish. But it was a lovely thing to hear. I thought about it all the time. After. After I had closed off both of our worlds.

25

The pub is one of those sloped stone rectangles that for reasons I will never understand has been pushed right up to the edge of the road. All this empty space and it chooses to spill its drunken customers out into the path of cars. Some sort of lesson in Darwinism there. A lone man stands outside. Pressed up against the wall. The tip of his cigarette burns orange in the gloom. He doesn't look up and the smoke pulls around his face.

I push open the door and the stale smell of beer and men slithers out. It's like stepping underground. Low lights and dark walls. Grey flagstone floor rolling away from me. Pitted with the weight of thousands of weaving drunken bodies over the years.

Nobody looks up at me. It's not one of those pubs. No pin-drop silence as the newcomer comes in. The interloper. Instead there's a studied lack of interest. Men clutch their pints and eye the TV screen. Horses running themselves to death. The girl behind the bar thumbs her phone. I approach her and she speaks directly to the screen

Yeah what do you want

It is impossible to tell if she's talking to me. I take a

chance. I order a lime soda and without taking her eyes off the phone she asks me if I want a single or double.

Of lime?

Oh she says and she looks up. It's hard to believe she's even old enough to work here. Her skin is so perfect that I am frozen by it. Almost translucent with youth. I can see the trace of veins at her temples. Streaks of blue in her hair and a handful of stars studded along the edges of her ears. *Sorry* she says and puts the phone on the sticky bar and then winces. *Just soda and lime? No vodka or anything?*

Just the lime and soda please. I shouldn't drink. When I drink I cannot keep a lid on the box. Oh the box. The box. The box the box the box.

The girl spurts soda from the siphon and searches for an ancient bottle of cordial. She inserts a straw and a browning crescent of lime with a flourish. I feel a squeeze of something in my chest.

Lime and soda she says and pushes it towards me. *Oh did you want ice? Sorry. I can add it now?*

It's fine I say. *It's absolutely great, thanks.*

I pay and take a sip and give her a grateful smile. She looks relieved. The lime and the fizz burn away the strange rotting taste in my mouth.

Did you see the sirens yesterday I ask her. *Hear about what happened on the marshes?* Her gaze has already slid off me. She is staring at her phone. I am not of interest to her.

I take the drink and I go and sit in the corner of the pub. Almost in total darkness and shadow. I lean against

63

the stone wall. It is slightly damp. I close my eyes and see her face. I stay there.

I start to fall asleep. I am so tired. It's as easy as breathing, hidden away in this dark corner. Just a few minutes. Just a little rest. Just close my eyes for a second.

I do not dream. It is so wonderful not to dream.

I jerk and twitch. My eyes wide open. For a moment I have no idea where I am. There is a flail of panic in my chest until I realise. I am embarrassed. A strange woman falling asleep in the corner of a pub. Is this what I have been reduced to now? But it probably isn't that strange here. I check my watch. Three hours. I have been asleep upright for three hours. I wipe my chin. Find a string of drool.

The pub door swings open and brings a sweeping arc of evening light. The heather wash of it makes me feel grimy. I take another sip of the lime soda to try to wake myself up. I think I should go back to the cottage. I get up and put the empty glass on the bar. The barmaid does not look up from her phone.

A group troops in. They bring the smell of the marshes with them. Walking boots. Anoraks. Waterproof trousers. Serious backpacks. Difficult haircuts. Their noise cuts through the gloom. They are excited, voices rising to the beamed ceiling. They crowd around the curve of the bar and the girl throws her phone a desperate glance. The screen dances with new messages.

Five pints of whatever's cheapest and on draught, love says a woman at the front. Lilting Welsh accent. Grey hair long and plaited in that impossible way I always worried about not being able to do. She has that kind of calm authority that I pretend comes with age but I know I will never have. She must be in her sixties but I can see the strength of her. Roped muscles in her forearms. Posture like a ballet dancer. I would put money on her doing yoga. I should do yoga. Her fingers are silvered with rings. Two on each finger, at least. Her nails are ragged and ringed with dirt and her hands are rough and dry. The rings are a strange moment of beauty. Of care. They circle her bones like little galaxies of jewels.

She sees me looking and offers me a smile that is all teeth and eyes. I immediately look away. That should be the end of that.

Not real of course she says and twists a silver ring scattered with huge blue stones. *But like my women might have worn. I like to think anyway. Little piece of them with me, you know. Bit of respect? They give me so much.*

I have no idea what this woman is talking about. I wonder if she might already be drunk. This thought gives me a bite of confidence. Drunk people talk easily.

Your women? I say. *Your . . .* I stop. Not sure of the right word. Not sure how to phrase this to show it's fine, it's obviously absolutely fine. I let the silence hang a little bit too long for that. She's going to hate me. I try anyway.

. . . partners? My voice rises up at the end. My mother hated that. Said it was from watching too much American

television. Tacky and unintelligent. I wonder if the care home leaves the TV on for her. I need to tell them not to do that. Maybe the radio, but not Classic FM. Radio 3 as long as it's not any of the religious bits. I wish I had thought to tell them earlier.

This woman throws back her head and laughs so loudly that the barmaid pulls her eyes from her phone. The sounds fill the dark of the pub. It is rich and soft and lovely. Some of the men turn from the hoofbeats of horses and stare.

My partners she repeats and there are tears in her voice. She nudges the man next to her. *Did you hear that, Hugo? Partners!* She waves her hands in front of his face and the laugh rises to the ceiling again.

I meet Hugo's eye and he raises his pint at me in a salute. He doesn't offer an explanation. There is foam on his top lip. He looks about twelve. He is wearing one of those fleeces with the huge breast pockets that London men wear when they cycle their fixie bikes or drink Japanese whisky from jam jars. It is dusty with mud.

Not my partners, love says the woman. She is wiping her eyes. *My women!* She is perhaps mad. Unaware she's just repeating the same information. Expecting a different understanding. I have a sudden flashbulb memory of my mother, pushing socks into the refrigerator. Telling me over and over that they weren't coming out clean. That everything smelled like garlic and old milk.

We're archaeologists offers Hugo quietly and finally. I hold this information for a moment. Try to pull together threads.

I can't. My head is swimming with the noise and strangeness of it all.

The women we find in digs says the woman. *All the ones I've ever worked with. That's my area, you see. Buried women. The ones forgotten in the earth. I like to remember them.* She holds out her hands towards me again. *So I have a ring made for every single one. Something they might have worn. This one* – she taps a twist of blackened silver that is scalloped along its edges – *is based on what she was actually wearing. So's this one.* She holds up her little finger. A faded gold loop. Patinaed and worn smooth. Something serpentine in the cling and curl of it. *But we're not always so lucky with that sort of thing. Usually I just have to imagine something for them. But it's nice, to carry something of them with me. They give me my life. I carry a bit of theirs.*

The barmaid puts down the final two pints. Two more anoraks grab them and the group looks around for a table.

And now I have another says the woman and the facts finally click into place like old clockwork. Cogs grinding and gnashing their teeth. *One more dead woman. One more story to tell. What a world, eh? What a fucked up, brilliant, awful, beautiful world.*

I stare at her. I just want her to keep talking. Keep telling me what she knows. Keep that voice rising to the beams and all around.

Join us says the woman and she doesn't pull her words up high at the end of her sentence. It is a statement.

67

And then I want to go back. I want to step outside into the inkdark and slip across the marsh. I want to be alone. I feel the tug of silence, of quiet, of nothingness.

I look at her hands. Ringed with death and stories.

Thank you I say and I take my lime and soda to the table in the corner.

26

Hugo gets me a pint. I fumble for a five-pound note. Find it slippery and fishlike in the inside pocket of my jacket. He won't take it. He pulls out my stool for me. I wonder if he has noticed my fingers are ringless.

Now we wait says the woman as Hugo balances my drink on the wobbling table and sits down with the fluid movements of a dancer. *Now we just have to wait. But we know, you just know. Just let the police do their little forms and exercise their box-ticking muscles. They'll clear off back to brutality and parking tickets tomorrow.*

A girl with a bullring in her nose clinks her pint glass with Hugo's.

Then we can help her says the woman. *We can uncover her. Uncover her body. Uncover her story. Remember her. Honour her.* She settles back and watches the young bodies around her. They are excited. Voices getting higher and wilder with every sip of beer.

What are the police doing I ask and the bullring girl rolls her eyes and mutters something about racial profiling and crimes against democracy. The woman gives her a soft smile.

The body Hugo says. He fiddles with a sliver of an earring in his right ear. I think it's some sort of animal tooth. Curved and lightly serrated. It has been accessorised with a small pale feather. Sharp and soft hanging together. I have a strange urge to bat it back and forth like a cat. *They have to check it's not a recent death. That's why the police have to come when someone finds human remains. To make sure it's not an active crime scene. Especially when they're so beautifully preserved. We do a bit of carbon dating, check how old the body really is. And this one is really old. We got sent the police photos yesterday and we knew. Jen pulled us off everything we were working on. Told us to get ready. We got the call this afternoon. They let us up there just now for the initial samples. But we already know the results will say it's really old. She is, I mean. Jen doesn't like it when we don't use proper pronouns when we know them. She is really old, we just know it. Not when she died though. Young then.* He stops speaking quite suddenly and goes red. He fiddles with the earring again. I wonder if the tooth is real.

What happened to her I say and the bullring girl juts her chin slightly. I feel like maybe I have stepped into a conversation that is not meant for me. But I take another sip of beer and feel it stream directly into my blood. I haven't had a drink in a very long time. I am warmed by it. I feel alive. This is a great idea. I can't believe I stopped doing this. I sip again.

Dunno yet says a man who has a trowel tattoo printed on his wrist. He reaches his hand out to shake mine. *Tom. Nice to meet you.* His grip is firm but not brutal. There is something sweetly boyish about him even though he is probably my age. He is not interested in leading the conversation. He is probably one of those people who listens. Says one incredibly insightful thing and then doesn't speak again all evening. I waste so many words.

Lilly says the bullring girl. She does not offer her hand. She gazes at me evenly. I give a weak little wave and hate myself.

The final anorak is Martin. He drains his pint and goes outside to smoke.

So you don't know what happened to her I ask.

We'll be able to find out says Hugo. He gazes right at me without blinking. I wonder if he has read something online about how to be intense and interesting to women. *Usually with the bog bodies they get buried away from the masses because of something shameful that they're meant to have done. Like they've been hidden away from the rest of their society. Buried all alone. A kind of shunning, I suppose. They might have got pregnant or had an affair or both. Sometimes they got sacrificed because of it. An offering to the gods to atone. Sometimes they died naturally and they were obviously then buried alone. I hope this one's a sacrifice.*

He sees me flinch and tries to smooth things. His cheeks are flushed again. He is so very young. I feel a thousand years old.

I mean like it's interesting from an anthropological perspective. I don't like, want her to have had a horrible death or anything. I don't like it when women are killed. I'm a feminist.

A man killed her says the bullring girl. She has finished

71

her pint. Her hands wrap around the glass. Her fingers are slender and her nails are painted violet.

How do you know that already I ask. I am impressed. Archaeologists have more tools at their disposal than the police.

It's always a man she says.

I can't think of much of an argument against that. Martin returns in a cloud of nicotine-drenched smoke and clinks his glass against Lilly's.

Hugo nods sombrely.

Societies were always killing women for whatever reasons suited them he says and I get the impression of a man warming to his subject. *It could vary from sect to sect. Sometimes what was fine in one group was verboten in another. So many different possibilities as to why they might have done it. Shame, honour, sacrifice for the greater good, for the gods or the weather or the harvest. Loads of different ways to do it as well. Poisoning them with hemlock or yew berries. Suffocation sometimes. Or cutting their throats or stabbing them in the heart with knives or sharp stones or axes. Really awful stuff.* Hugo adds the last sentence as some sort of apology for his eager scamper through murder methods. He lowers his eyes. Mourning all the long-dead women with low-lashed reverence. Listing their deaths like a menu. I cradle his words. All these ways to die. There are yew trees in the park. I add it to the list. I wonder if JP will creep out one night and pluck the berries from the branches. Throw them into the sewer grates. Keep me safe in his impossible way.

Hugo is still talking about death.

But the question says Jen, as she cuts through Hugo's one-man requiem *is why she came up?*

Hugo and the girl share a glance that does not include me.

Came up? I watch Jen's fingers as they flutter along her pint glass.

Through the soil Jen says. *By herself. To face the world. Usually, when we get called in it's because a machine or a person has done some digging. Sometimes a dog. But generally they're discovered roughly where they've always been. Peat cutters used to find they'd sliced off an arm somewhere three feet below. The earth moves them, of course. But right up? No. Our geophysicists will have a look but I know the answer already. Archaeology is the dead talking to the living. Some people think that's just a metaphor. I don't — Hugo, stop rolling your eyes, you're an egg. I don't think it's a metaphor at all. She's talking to us. She's going to talk to us. She came up for something. She came looking. I can feel it. She wants something.*

I am suddenly sticky with the heat of the pub. My armpits prickle with damp. Jen is mad. Of course she's mad. I should have known she'd be mad. But I want to believe her. I do believe her. The heat within me is roaring to a burn. The beer sludges through my blood. The face. The face in the mud. The face looking at me. The face I knew. The truth of what Jen is saying spikes hard and sure. She is looking. She wants something. It is ridiculous and absurd and fantastical and it is true. I know it is true. I am going mad too. It's about time.

Looking? I manage.

Yes. Looking for something. Existing. Sentient. You can't get tied down to what we think about death, the dead, the afterlife. Now, maybe, when we die we just die and rot away to nothing. Or maybe we burn in the fire of hell or rise up to some lovely cloudy utopia and sit at that one God's knee. Those are the ideas these days, right? But these bodies aren't bound by our beliefs. They exist in their own time. And that time was full of myth and hauntings and wanderings and sacrifice and blood and gods and ghosts and revenge. So why on earth wouldn't she be here for a reason? Her own reason. And why would she push her way up if she wasn't trying to find something? Someone?

I order three bottles of red wine for the table and drink a large glass in one bloody gulp.

27

Clouds of conversation drift past me. Patterns of words that are familiar but have no meaning to me.

Carbon dating

Stratum

Back dirt

Midden

Soil analysis

Soil matrix

Faunal remains

It's like poetry.

28

The inevitable question rises to the surface.

What are you doing here then

Jen twists the serpentine ring around her little finger and looks right at me. Her question pulls the rest of the group into a lull of quiet. I feel stripped away. Bare. I want to tell her everything and I think she already knows it all anyway. Her eyes are bright blue.

Writing a book

Hugo moves closer towards me.

I'd love to do that—

What are you writing about Jen asks. She shifts her body slightly. Pushing her shadow over Hugo as he opens his mouth and then closes it again. He takes a sip of pint and finds nothing but foam. I need to pee but I don't want to break the circle. Don't want to step out of Jen's gaze.

I don't know I say and the truth of it feels like a burn. I want to give her something. I want her to think I carry stories with me too. That I know what I'm doing. That I'm not just some idiot with a notebook and a freight train of emotional baggage. *That's the point I suppose. Find something here. Or just be in a new space I guess.*

Jen claps her hands together in delight. *An archaeologist* she crows. *That's what you are. Just waiting until you find something. Or until it finds you, although this lot think I'm mad when I say that. Go to the bar, Hugo. Wine again, I think. Take my card.*

I try to protest but Jen silences me with another flap of her hands. She seems to be able to conduct all of life through the flick of her fingers, the movement of her palms. I think of my mother, constantly plucking at nothing. In charge of no one. Stories all forgotten.

Why women I ask her as she pours more wine into our red-silted glasses. Jen looks at me.

Oh I suppose I could tell you something about women being the source of all life. About the power of the female body. About the treatment of that body through the ages. About wanting to discover their stories. All that. She stops talking. I was expecting another sentence.

Is it not that? I ask. I am nervous for a reason I cannot articulate.

It is she says. *Of course it is. That's why I do it. But we always have our own selfish reasons too, don't we?*

I don't know how to respond. But Jen isn't looking for a response. She sips her wine.

The voices of the rest of the group rise up and around us like the sea and I am swept up in their noise and their chatter. I sip my wine and I listen to the details of their day. The call from the police. The samples taken. The wait for results. The anticipation of something extraordinary.

We order chips and the oil spills into the whorls of my fingerprints and I lick salt from my thumbs. Flavour bursts for the first time in months. I eat one, two, three. Hugo and the bullring girl argue about sample collections. Jen listens as Martin and I talk. I have miscast him as a gruff and surly man but he expands in front of me. He talks about art, music, the galleries he visits whenever he gets to go abroad on digs. He reads the Booker Prize shortlist every year and I feel like a fraud. He is earnest. He wants my opinion on this year's winner. He loved it. He could see why other people didn't. I tell him I haven't read it. That I'm catching up on my reading pile. *I know that feeling* he says. He tells me he read my first novel. This never happens. We talk about authorial intent and experimental structures and unlikeable protagonists and I quietly realise he is not talking about my book at all. After a while he realises too. We don't say anything. We politely finish the discussion and he turns away to talk to Tom.

But of course says Jen as she drains her wine glass. *You must write about her.*

For a second I am caught frozen in her words and I think

I can't

And I am pulled under with panic and horror at the thought of shaping that

And then the waves crash around us again and I understand.

Yes I think. I could try that, couldn't I?

29

You should all come for dinner I say and the wine is in charge of my mouth. *Tomorrow. Come to the cottage. I'll cook.* I am really drunk. *Come round and eat and talk. A dinner party.*

I don't do dinner parties. I've only got Pot Noodles and plastic cheese.

Jen keys her number into my phone and hands hers over for me to do the same. I stumble over the order of my fingers on the screen. The wine is heavy in my blood.

There's no signal here I say stupidly and Jen sighs and squints at her phone. *Wondered why I didn't get a call yet* she says and she holds it up to the ceiling. There must be internet at the pub. The barmaid and her Instagram addiction. I didn't think to check. I didn't want to know what my phone might tell me. I could join the Wi-Fi now. Send JP a message. Call the home and check that my mother is still alive. I take my phone back from Jen and slip it into my pocket. It is nearly out of battery anyway. I always used to wonder whether when my mother dies, I will feel something. A snap of a connection. The invisible cord that has always looped and stretched between us. That I will just know she is gone and I am unmoored.

I don't think that any more. Death is slippery and unbe-
lievable.

When she dies I will not know.

I did not even know when the cord slipped from me.

Come and find us tomorrow Jen says. *She'll be ours by then.
Just come and find us. And then we can get directions for dinner.*

Dinner. Yes. I said that. Ten or eleven seconds ago.

I walk home alone because I cannot call the taxi driver
and let his chatter pierce through me. I run through the
possible outcomes. Murder. Cardiac arrest. Hit by a car.
Ditchdeath. Wolves. Lovely stuff.

The world is tilting and moonlit. I reach my hands out
and brush them against the dark. I look up and I see the
stars biting through the black. When my father died my
teacher told me he was a star in the sky now. I asked which
one and she said whichever was the brightest. *That's Daddy*
she said and there were tears in her eyes and none in mine.
I was just confused. *The brightest one, that's Daddy's star* she
said and she held my shoulders tightly. *I thought he was
buried in the ground* I said. She gave me a lollipop from her
special drawer and didn't answer. It was cherry flavoured
so I traded it with Sarah W for a rubber shaped like an ice
cream cone. I asked my mother that evening and she laughed
and said Daddy was definitely just dead in the ground and
not the sky. *Which is a lot more bloody use* she said and
pointed out through the window at the black night. *You
can't see a single bloody star in London. Anyway, imagine how
that would possibly work? Everyone dead is somehow the brightest*

star in the sky? Think about it. How could everyone be the brightest? Doesn't make sense, Anna, does it? I shook my head. I thought something had sounded off.

My mother was very practical about death.

I can always find Orion's Belt. That's it. Three sartorial stars. I looked through the telescope at Greenwich Observatory on a school trip when I was younger. I didn't expect to see some asteroid version of my father floating through the cosmos. I wanted to see a sky full of animals like the stories promised. But they weren't there. Just stars, lone and ranging. Even when I looked at a map of the constellations, I still couldn't understand how those pinprick dots joined up made a bear or a hunter or a vengeful crab.

They could have been anything at all.

30

I am just so very drunk. I realise how bad it is in a rush that tastes like hops and red wine. I am not used to alcohol now. I am not used to drinking with young people with piercings and tattoos that aren't heavily associated with choices made and regretted in the mid-to-late 2000s. I am not used to being able to think about something else for fragments of an evening.

The tarmac beneath my feet is surprising and solid. I lurch anyway. The road gets away from me. I can't catch it. I stumble and my knees hit the grey ground and the shock of it rings through me and my stomach jerks and there is a rush of spit and sick. I vomit. It is unexpected and violent. My fingers grip the ground. I raise my head and see the stars.

I retch red wine and it spreads and twists like blood on the asphalt. Like I'm bringing up my insides. Turning myself inside out. Coughing up rot. Saliva strings from my mouth. I strain and stretch until nothing comes up. Bile burning its way out of me. I close my eyes and I see her face in the blackness of my eyelids.

Oh the box the box the box.

Wine always brings it out of me.

God, love, you all right

I look up. Bleary. Slick with sweat. Wipe my mouth with my sleeve. A shadow shaped against the sky. A car tucked into a passing place. Hazard lights blinking ticktock ticktock. Staining the road orange.

It's the bloody taxi driver.

Does no one else live here?

I lift a hand. Fine, fine. All good here. Just a little road-side puke. Can't complain.

Do you need a lift somewhere love and he jangles his keys awkwardly in one hand.

My face must shift.

No charge love. I'm heading your way anyway. The cottage, yes?

I don't want to get into his car and smell his new-car-smell Christmas tree air freshener and veer round the country bends with my hands gripping the door handle.

But I don't want to walk either. I am trapped. Don't want to go forward or back. Can't stay here.

I haul myself up. Stumble to the taxi. He pulls open the door for me. Lets me slide into the backseat without a word. I don't pull my seatbelt across and he doesn't say anything. He rolls the window down a little. Cold air on my cheek.

We pull away. He drives slowly. Takes each bend with care. The tenderness of it hollows me out. I rest my fore-head against the cool glass of the window. Can't bear to watch the landscape slide by. It streams like a ribbon. Can't make it steady itself. Close my eyes.

Here you go love he says and his voice is terrible and soft and I hold myself still. *Get yourself some ginger biscuits. They always help my missus, at the beginning.*

I throw open the door and I drag myself from the car and I make it to the verge just in time and blackness spills from inside me. I see the white of masticated chips speckling the sedge.

I wave the taxi on. His eyes fix on me in the rear-view mirror as he drives away. He doesn't want to leave me by the side of the road. I give a brief nod. I'm all right. I'm all right.

My stomach is empty and the wine sludge has shifted from my blood. My thoughts are sharper but I feel scooped out and hollow. My mouth is puckered and dry. I need water. I can't remember the last time I had a glass of water. JP bought me one of those bottles with motivational messages on the side. Keep it up! Keep drinking! Hydrate yourself! Fill me up and go again! He thought it was sweet and encouraging. I dropped it in the hospital car park and I was so pleased when the plastic caught on a stone and cracked.

31

I drink water in the dark. The moonlight pools in the glass. My hands look pale and bare.

I think of Jen's storied fingers. I used to wear a ring.

JP and I met in a restaurant. I had given up on Hinge and Tinder and Bumble. Slick marketing names hiding the horror of a thousand men who just wanted something blank-eyed and smiling to fuck. Whenever I told them about my mother, which I always did fast and early like a litmus test as to how much of a cunt they were going to turn out to be, they would inch away from me. This one's not worth it. I could see the thought pass across their faces.

I went for dinner with friends on a Friday instead. Just a small place near my smaller flat. Low lighting and lovely chairs. The food was good. Great, actually. The music was low but tasteful. I stayed afterwards with a book and a glass of something oily and overpriced. Turned off my phone in case my mother rang. JP worked behind the bar. Or that's what I thought. He sent me a little bowl of crispy beignets. Clouded soft with sugar and stuffed with smooth raspberry. I ate them with my fingers and avoided his eye. I wondered if you could deep fry date rape drugs. JP came over to ask if I wanted another glass of the wine. Perhaps he could recommend something better. On the house. I liked his accent. I asked him the way to the bibliothèque. He laughed. He took off his apron and sat with me. We talked. I told him about my mother. She had just gone into the home. The carers couldn't come frequently enough to keep her safe. I couldn't move in and look after her. I should have tried. I was tortured with the guilt and relief of it. She hadn't wanted to go. It was the best place for her. She didn't understand. She screamed and tried to bite me and wept every time I visited. JP asked her name. No one had ever done that. I stayed. I told him about her and I didn't make it into a joke. I was tender. I said all the things I'd left too late to tell her. JP listened. We covered all of our worlds and the evening spun on and on. He taught me how to swear in French. I taught him how to roll a pound along his knuckles. My only party trick. He was useless at first. The coin pinged to the floor and I got a head rush picking it up time after time. He got it eventually and the look of joy on his face made me want to love him. It was stupid and silly and it was so much fun. I asked him if he'd get in trouble for clocking off early. He laughed again. Easy and fluid. He owned the whole place. Him and his silent partner. *Not so silent* he said and that laugh again.

God I miss it.

32

I wear the darkness like a cloak. I am alone and invisible out here. I stand on the very edge of the marsh and the line of the land stretches far away. There is no end. No horizon stitching itself to the ground. I could walk forever and be in the same place all over again. The moonlight is puddling across the water and the earth is turned to mercury. I could sink straight through.

I step forward. My foot plunges. I am not wearing my boots. Not even my socks. I must have forgotten. My feet are pearly in the silver light. I don't feel the cold or the numb of the bog water. I feel nothing at all and it is perfect. I step again. I sink into the biting ground. My ankle is held firm. The earth wants to swallow me whole and I can let it. I twist and pull, just to see if it will let me go. There is no moment of release. No sucking gloopy belch as the wet ground spits me out. But I can step again. I can keep walking. But each step pulls me further into the belly of the bog.

I can stay still. Frozen on the surface of this world. Unmoving. Unearthed.

I can keep going.

I can be pulled under.

Nothing but the beautiful dark.

The undertow of roots and animal.

I step again.

The bog howls.

A language I can speak.

Up to my knees up to my waist up to my breasts.

life and death and mud and milk

My neck.

Dirt like hands around me

Clawing

My chin my mouth my nose

Bubbling water for breath

Mud and silt and nothing.

My eyes.

My eyes my eyes my eyes.

Pressed against the darkness.

Skimming the soil.

Under under under

Let me drown let me drown let me drown

A face

Caught in the water

Pewter

Rosebud mouth

Lines made by root and worm and sun and dark

Eyes open in the halfdark

Lashes spiked with soil

Staring back

Silted mirror
I know her I know her I know her.
That terrible beautiful mouth
Opens
A rush of earth and rot and the scuttle of insects
And a sound that hollows my bones
I know it
It is mine
It belongs to her

She is keening
Griefsong
And dirt and loss and horror and soil and death
And black
Always shifting black

33

I wake and I am still trapped. I fight the white sheets that are tying me to the bed. Push myself to the surface. Gasping for air. My hair is curled and slick with sweat. Salt on my skin. The dream has left its tide marks on my body. Grief and death and things lost forever. I can see the shapes of it behind my eyelids. I want to wash it all off. Scrub it all away.

I can taste the bitter silt of the bog and I scrape my tongue along my teeth. I go to the bathroom and spit into the sink. I half expect to see black earth streaking the greying porcelain. The slither of an earthworm shivering pinkly towards the plughole. I could crumble to mud and silt and dirt right now. Let it pour from my bones. My flesh is black.

No. I am unbelievably hungover. Every cell sucked dry by alcohol. My skull is as fragile as an egg. My eyeballs are bruised. My mouth feels pickled. My tongue a foreign object. I drink water from the tap. Feel the ice of it flood my tender stomach. Splash it on my saltmarked face.

I can't face the plunge and pull of a bath. I settle for a flannel and the cracked basin instead. I am proud of myself for keeping clean and tidy. Just like my mother always said. Clean and tidy and ready to face the day. *Once you're dressed, you can do anything* she said to me once when I was a teenager and wearing ironic Hello Kitty pyjamas all day every day. I laughed and ignored her then but sometimes her words swirl back to me now. I pull a brush through my hair and scrunch it into a knot at the base of my neck. Tie it with a rubber band. Hear my mother telling me it will tear my hair, give me split ends, ruin the curl. I don't look in the mirror. Make a black coffee and a sachet of golden syrup porridge in the microwave. Push it round with a teaspoon. It steams and then gives up and congeals. Great oaty clots greying in the bowl. I scrape it into the bin. Why bloody bother. JP would make it properly, slowly. An iron pan and a lot of double cream. Never water. That was only for people who hated themselves. Big heaping spoonfuls of brown sugar. A splash of whisky if it was the weekend. Single malt only. Never a blend, even in porridge. I didn't even know the difference until I met JP. It all tasted like a mouthful of hospital air to me. But he spent his first UK years in Scotland. He could find the notes and flavours as easy as breathing. Sometimes I catch the burr in his accent and I think about what it would have been like if he'd stayed up there. If he'd found a lovely girl in Edinburgh and settled down in one of those tenement flats with the windows and the light streaming in and an accepted level of damp in the walls. If he'd got married in a kilt. Her brothers hilariously wearing berets at the reception. A little joke between family. Bagpipes and baguettes. Big Christmases with a whole carpet of brightly wrapped presents. Children tearing them open wildly. Chocolate smeared on their pink-cheeked faces. A red bow stuck on the dog's collar. A baby dressed as a reindeer, with handfuls of paper clenched tightly in fat fists.

The box the box the box oh god the box.

In the hospital I told him I wished we'd never met. It was just after. We had been left alone. The door was tightly closed. It had some sort of secret sign or symbol on it. I can't remember what it was. Oh. A plastic flower. Something that should have been alive but was just a waxy copy of the real thing. So that the staff would know. Wouldn't say something *insensitive*. They had put us somewhere as far away as possible from everything going on but I could still hear everything outside. The cries fresh from new lungs. It was almost comical. I wondered if I would ever tell the story and laugh. *Can you believe it? We could hear everything! What are they like, eh? Bloody NHS!* Then we'd all have a big drink of a mid-price red wine and say something serious about how they were doing the best they could in the economic circumstances and terrible government cuts and would anyone like the cheeseboard now?

Lying in the metal-sided bed in a gown softened by the wash and wear of a thousand other bodies, the morphine and the blood loosened my tongue. I painted the scenes for him. The girl and the flat and the wedding and the kilt and the Christmas and the baby. I stared at the polystyrene ceiling tiles and I didn't look at him once. He told me to be quiet. When I wouldn't stop he told me to shut up. JP had never raised his voice to me. It wasn't his way. He shouted the words now. I kept going. He beat his fist against the arm of the chair and the sound shocked me into silence.

He sat in the high-backed chair and it wasn't the picture I wanted to see. I closed my eyes. He wanted me to look. I could see everything projected onto the insides of my eyelids like a cinema screen. He begged me. He said she was beautiful and perfect and that I actually did laugh at that. I couldn't look. Instead I carried on telling him about the whole new life I had made for him. I hadn't fucked this one up. I wasn't part of it at all. It was so much better, wasn't it? Wouldn't it be better? He said he didn't want it. He was lying. He didn't shout again. He cried and he said this was what he wanted, every awful fucking second of it. I told him to get out.

I stop the memory.

No more.

34

I find my way back to the site easily. I am maybe starting to understand the landscape. I can see the lines and lean of the earth. The paths emerge like hidden streams and I follow them without thinking.

The day is clear and the sky is wide and blue. There are no clouds painted on the water. Squint sideways and you could believe you were somewhere hot and bright. A sliver of the Mediterranean in the marshes.

My mouth is dry and my palms sweat. I clench my slippery fists and my fingernails make half-moons in my skin. I am nervous of it all. Of seeing Jen. Of seeing the body. Of finding my part in this. I don't think I have a part in it. I can't stay away. I have brought a notebook and a pen. I feel like an idiot. JP would have baked brownies with studs of white chocolate and a twist of salted caramel running fatly through the middle. He never turns up anywhere without a Tupperware box. When my university friend Nina had a baby he filled her freezer. Every box carefully labelled in his ridiculous French penmanship, all curls and slants and impossible Rs. Consistent as a computer. They really get handwriting right in French schools. Six minutes in the microwave, stir once. Oven-bake at 180, 40 minutes. *God you're so bloody lucky* Nina said. She was lying on the sofa scattering oat biscuit crumbs over the head of her newborn. He was all scrunched up like a frog. Little skinny limbs and whorls of hair that looked like they could have been painted on. Jonah. I was the whale. Nina picked a flake of chocolate from the perfect curl of his ear and popped it into her mouth. *So bloody lucky. He'll be a brilliant dad you know. And actually even if he's crap you'll be well-fed. I think I'd probably choose that, on balance. Andy can't even make pasta.*

I haven't seen Nina since before. She has given up sending messages into silent space. Jonah will be walking now. I didn't remember his birthday.

35

The site is very different today. There are white-suited ghosts padding between tents. Cameras slung round their necks, complicated machines clutched in their hands. The blue tent is still pitched high over the space where I saw her last. It looks alien and ridiculous. Something so modern and plasticky set up in an ancient world. There is also a smaller white tent gaping open at the mouth. Hugo emerges from it. There is a steaming paper cup in his hand. He waves at me. Beckons me over.

It's the author! Morning! You heard then he says and takes a sip from the cup. He pulls a face. *Always terrible coffee on a dig. I'll never get used to it. They say it's not instant but it's so obviously instant, you know?*

Heard what I say and I follow him back into the tent. Inside are two small tables. One of them is covered in trowels and tools. The other is weighed down by a couple of metal urns and a tray of thickly-margarined sandwiches. The air smells like coffee and ham.

That it's not a murder says Hugo and he gestures between the urns. *Well, not one the police are interested in anyway. Bit too much of a cold case for them. By about three thousand years.*

Ha. Anyway just like we knew it would be. Jen always knows. Tea or coffee?

Coffee please I say. *Definitely coffee, it's so early.* It's not really. Not for people with jobs and lives and purpose. My head pulses.

Hugo hands me a paper cup. It is definitely instant. I don't care. It's incredibly strong. I drink half of it in one go. It helps.

How did she die I say. I wonder if I should get my note-book out. I have no idea what I would write.

Hugo takes another sip of coffee and grimaces. He shrugs.

We don't know that yet. Not until we've seen the whole of her. Sometimes that shows you, with a body that well preserved. Sometimes it's the tests that tell you. Feels like we should place bets, really. Axe or knife? Baby or hemlock?

I feel a prickle of irritation. Her life was real. Her death was real. Hugo sees my face ripple.

Just a joke he says. *You have to have a bit of black humour. Like doctors, you know what I mean? What do they call it? Gallows humour. Keeps you sane.*

Jen is beside me. Her hand on my elbow.

Come and see her darling she says. *Come and see her. She's waiting.*

We move away from the stink of the sandwiches and the burnt coffee and Hugo running his hands through his hair.

Just a child says Jen and for a moment I think she's talking about the body but then I realise she means Hugo. *Just a*

97

child. He's very clever though. In all the wrong ways at the moment, but he'll learn. They always do. When they're with me.

Jen's rings catch the sunlight. I feel magpielike. I want to pluck at them. Hold them. Hoard them. Slide them onto my own fingers and feel the cool weight of them. I run my thumb along the smooth skin of the ring finger on my left hand. The gold band is in my bedside table drawer. I put it on top of the box. I didn't do it deliberately. But it seems neat now. The symbols of that section of my life carefully packaged together. Shut away.

Jen gives me a papery white suit to pull on over my clothes. She passes me elasticated shoe covers to snap over my boots and I rustle as I kneel down. My vision spots and blackens just for a second as I stand up. Sweat is already pooling in the small of my back. The suit traps the heat from my body and holds it close to me.

And a mask says Jen. I adjust the straps around my ears and think back to the moment I wanted to reach out and cradle the dark face in my bare hands. Just a flash of madness.

Through here says Jen and we duck under the flaps of the blue tent and the light it casts on the ground is marine and eerie. I am swallowed by it. Underwater. The dream flares on my skin.

You can go now Lilly. Jen speaks to the bullring girl and then gestures at the tent flap. The suit has made her anonymous and alien but I can still see her hands. There is a comfort in them.

Lilly nods and rustles out of the tent entrance. I hear the

rasp and crunch of her suit being pulled off. Hugo is offering her a coffee and asking her something about chemicals.

Now there is nobody else in here except us and her. The noise of the archaeologists and their unhappiness with the quality of the coffee and the lack of oat milk fades to nothing.

The body has low string ropes all around her. Just her face is visible, like before. Peering up at the plastic blue sky. She is exactly as I remember her. Exactly as she was last night in the blurred underworld of my dream. I'm glad she is the same. I don't want her to change. I don't want anything to happen to her while I'm not here. I want to be here.

I know you.

The thought again. The maddening wild and stupid thought sharp in my brain. The same urge to reach out and hold her. Find her hand under all the layers of dirt and lace my fingers through it. Press my cheek to hers. Tell her I understand.

Her mouth is open. Like there are words waiting for me.

I know you.

A flutter of air and breath. I lean closer. I want to listen. But there is only quiet and still.

Now I am closer I can see she is changed. She is different. There is a powdery texture to her face now. I wonder with a heartsink sickness whether she is starting to rot. I can't stand the thought. But as I peer in I can

99

see that whatever is on there has been spread and brushed on. It is alien. It is not a part of her in the way rot would be. I hate it.

Her skin I say and my voice is muffled by the mask. All my words are kept so close to my mouth. *What have you done to her? What's happened to her?* I sound sharper than I intended. They have changed her. They have touched her. They are interfering. This is not how it should be. This is not how she should be. I have no right to say these things. I have no right to be angry. But I cannot help it. It is an instinct that forces its way through my body. The pathways are smooth with use.

We've brushed her with anoxic compounds says Jen. She is crouching low. Gazing at the woman. Something in her gaze softens me. I relax my body, my lungs. *To stop the oxygen degrading her. The bog has held her. Kept her preserved and perfect. As soon as the air touched her, she started to break down. We're against the clock, really. Exhume her carefully, get our sampling done, make sure she doesn't degrade any further. Imagine, dying in 1200 BCE and still having skin on your bones, teeth in your head, heart in your chest.*

1200 BCE. I could never work out dates. Numbers always spooled away from me. My mother said I read too many words to pay attention to maths. It made some sense at the time. Stories were better than equations. But now sometimes I am caught by it and I feel stupid and stuck. Like there's a language being spoken around me and I can't find my way into the conversation.

Something must show in the strip of my face visible above the mask.

She's from the Iron Age says Jen quietly. She looks at that burnt stone face with a tenderness that pierces me. *Carbon dating. She's been in the ground all that time. What a life. What a death.*

I can smell death. I wish I'd brought some water with me. The tent is so very hot. The air sticks to me. The scent of the bog wraps itself around me. It is thick and rich. The paper suit traps the heat of my body close to my skin and I pull at the seams around my neck.

The air is clotting around me. There isn't enough oxygen. My mask is smothering me. I can't take in breaths deep enough to keep my brain clear and sharp.

Step out for a minute Jen says. *Get some water. We'll be here when you're ready. We need to get started.*

36

I pull the mask from my face and suck bright air into my lungs. It feels euphoric. I wonder for a moment whether the body had the same feeling when her face pushed out of the earth. The clawing sink and stink of the mud replaced by the world above. The fresh air and the old sky. I wonder whether it will feel even better to be lifted from the ground entirely. Exhumed. That was the word Jen had used. It is cold, distant. I wonder whether being pulled out of the earth will be a release. A relief. Or whether it will feel like she is being torn away. Torn apart.

Jen brings me a plastic bottle of lukewarm water and I drink it in one go. The plastic crunches and crumples as I pull at the last few drops.

It can be a lot says Jen. *When you see something like that. But I think everyone should see death. Especially if they're a writer, an artist. If you're a writer, you write about life. You write about death. You have to look it in the eye. You know Géricault? The painter.* The Raft of the Medusa. *That wonderful, awful painting. All those men, dying, drowning, starving, eating each other. That wasn't pulled straight from Géricault's head. He visited morgues. To study the colour of the dead. To know them. The pull and pallor of their skin, the whites of their eyes, the blue of their nails. And look at that result. Art that will live forever. From gazing upon death.*

A trickle of water escapes into my lungs and I cough. Jen pats my back. She moves her hand in slow circles like a mother winding a baby. Her fingers brush and catch on the cotton reels of my spine. I hold the shrunken bottle tight.

I don't know what's wrong with me I say even though of course I do.

We're going to start the dig now Jen says softly. *You can watch, but you need to keep clear of the work. I think you'll find it interesting. It'll be very busy. And we'll have to work fast. Remember what I said about how the air will decay her. We're going to find out her story. Her life. Her death. And you'll look at the dead and write her. Imagine, a book about her. About one of my women.*

It has not been agreed that I will write a book about the body. About her. I have this sort of conversation a lot. People telling me they have a story for me. A book that needs to be written. They never do. Very occasionally they have an anecdote that could probably be massaged into a few paragraphs and tucked away in the corners of another book. The whole architecture and structure of an actual novel is missing. I always nod politely and thank them for sharing. Sometimes at parties I just say I work in an accountant's office. It is boring enough that nobody ever asks any follow-up questions. Everybody just makes the same tired joke about whether I can do their tax returns. As the gap between my first book and the expected follow-up widened, I started telling the lie for different reasons.

I mean I might use her as a starting point I say weakly but Jen has already walked back towards the blue tent with a line of archaeologists following her like paper-clad duck-lings.

37

The trench is begun a metre away from the body. To stop the tip of a spade slicing through a leg and to make sure they collect as much earth as possible. It will all be searched through. For anything she was buried with or anything that will tell them more. It will all be recorded in numbers and charts and photographs. The whole scene is efficient and precise. I hate it. There is chatter about the chemical toilets arriving and whether the proper catering will come in time or if someone will have to drive to the shop. All the sandwiches have been eaten. They were made by a woman in the back of the pub and nobody liked them. There weren't any vegan options.

They will dig far deeper than the body. They will put all the soil into heaps and buckets. They will load her onto a stretcher and carry her away to be preserved and studied. They will leave nothing but the bare empty earth that held her tight for so long. Soon she will vanish from this space. Exhumed. Excised. Removed from the world that has known her for thousands of years.

There is a terrible sadness about it. It hangs like a cloud. I wonder if they can all feel it too. I want to ask. I don't know how to ask.

The dig itself is not interesting after about five minutes. I find that a bit embarrassing to admit. I should be fascinated. Seeing this strange thing that hardly anyone ever gets to witness. Being part of history, art, science. But it is boring. It is hot. The forensic suits and the plastic roof and the body-heat coalesce into a temperature that quickly becomes unbearable. They are working with deep concentration against a constant fine spray of water and dirt. I am always in the way. I shift my body into ever smaller shapes and spaces and I am still interrupting the rhythm of the work. I spill a bucket of soil and Hugo has to scrape it all up again. I whisper that I'm sorry but the words are lost in my mask.

They are still far away from the edges of the body. They stop every few minutes to look at images on iPads. Some sort of underground scans that direct them where to lift the earth from. It is all so slow. Jen said the dig would be fast. I am bored and hungover. My legs ache from standing and crouching and contorting myself into invisibility every time the archaeologists shift positions. I need to pee. My bladder twitches. The toilets have not yet arrived. Neither has the catering.

Lilly is told to drive to the shop. I want to object on her behalf. She is the youngest. A woman. This shouldn't be how things still are.

I'll go with you is what I actually say.

38

Lilly drives with the precision of a drunk. I am thrilled by it. Each bend seems to be a 50/50 chance of life or death. I like the odds. She rolls down the window and vapes. The strawberry clouds whip straight back into the car. She offers the vape to me and the car veers wildly. I take it and I am surprised by the force of the nicotine rush. I blink away black spots.

I'm sorry they made you go and get the lunch I say and she looks at me. The car weaves onto the right-hand side of the road. There are complicated lines and arrows inked onto the soft undersides of her wrists. I wonder if Lilly once tried to die. If she is braver than I am.

It was my turn she says and her words are strawberry scented. *It's not sexism. Or I wouldn't have gone.* She gives me a pitying look. She knows everything. She is perhaps twenty-one.

That's good I mumble and I spend the rest of the journey imagining the car spinning through the sky and landing in the marshes. Vanishing without a trace. Sinking into the bogworld. Lovely.

Lilly parks at an impossible angle and opens the driver's

side door before she's turned the engine off. Everything smells like burnt rubber and petrol. I don't go to the shop with her. She is spiky with me. I wonder if she likes Hugo and thinks he likes me. I think about telling her I'm married. I don't. I tell her I'm going to the pub. Inside I ask the same teenage barmaid for the Wi-Fi password. She recites it like a prayer.

I ask the barmaid for a double lime and soda and she looks at me blankly. I am already forgotten, folded into the shadowy corners of the pub like the anonymous men dotted on stools in the gloom. I sit at a table with the drink and the glow of the racing behind me. I feel unsettled. Untethered. The feeling wraps around me. Takes root.

My phone connects for the first time in days. I am tense, fingers curled around the edges of the screen. I wait for the bad news. The missed calls from the home. The voice-mails from JP. *I'm sorry, ma chérie, I'm so sorry, I tried to call you, but she's gone.* The sucking panic that everything is over, once again. The last strings cut. Unmoored. I wonder about the ways I will miss her.

There are no calls. No voicemails. Emails and WhatsApps flutter through. I am surprised JP hasn't tried to call. We said he shouldn't. But I thought he would.

An email from my editor. She hopes it's all going well. Don't forget to send a headshot for the literary fund's website. Is the delivery date still all right? Anything I'd like to send along, just for her to have a look at? Anything at all. Just a couple of pages would be perfect! Even a vague outline?

My oldest friend Lucy sends me a photo of an echidna and asks if I knew that they have four-headed penises. *But they can only use two heads at one time, so what's the point? Men are so half-arsed. Half-penised. Love you!*

Lucy went to my secondary school and on the first day she sat next to me and said we would probably end up being friends so we might as well start now. She didn't like reading books or writing poetry the way I did, but she also didn't like P.E. or wearing industrial quantities of lip gloss so she was a loser too. We used to eat our homemade sandwiches in the corner of the dining hall and pretend we didn't want to be part of that group anyway.

She hasn't given up on me but we don't talk about anything serious. She was the first person to ask me if there was something wrong with my mother. Everyone else politely ignored the problem until I came to them with the facts, the diagnosis. Then they nodded like they'd always known. They just hadn't wanted to get involved. The diagnosis was twelve years ago. There had been problems for years before that though. Just small things. The kind of things where you look back and realise. But at the time it's just a moment. A small, strange moment in a sequence of normal ones. Forgetting a word. Not remembering the next stage when she was making a cup of tea. Frozen with the mug in one hand, the idea of a teabag whistled out of her brain. I had gone away to university and every time I came home my mother was a degree further away from normal. She was somehow a stronger version of herself and altogether different at the same time. All of her traits dialled up. I asked her to see a doctor and she laughed so much that I left the room. I left university and found a flat. It didn't occur to me to come home and take care of her. Sometimes I wonder if I am missing something too. The gene for care. For nurture. If there is a badness in me that meant I got what I deserved.

I went round twice a week. I corrected the mistakes she made around the house. I turned off the hob and pulled the carton of milk out of the washing machine. I let her tell me the same stories over and over again. It was nice, sometimes. She talked about my father. She sometimes thought she was talking *to* my father. I let her pretend. I listened as she told me about a disastrous walking holiday in the Yorkshire Dales. About the time the bath overflowed and the water crashed through the ceiling. About how he would be sad if he saw a single glove abandoned on the pavement. That was me, I said. I was the one who got sad about the glove. She looked right through me. I went back to my flat and wondered whether the fire brigade would call and say the house had burned to a crisp.

I took her to the doctor by lying to her. She was furious but she couldn't show it in front of a medical professional. She always respected people in jobs like that. Diagnosis is tricky, the doctor said. She made a referral. But I already knew what was going to happen. The specialist did scans and tests. Drew empty clock faces for my mother to fill in. I watched her bunch all of the numbers into one quarter of the circle and I didn't cry. The specialist said she could have five years, she could have twenty. It was early onset. That made it more difficult to predict. So who could say? My mother told him to fuck off. She had slipped even further. It had only been a month.

A week after the diagnosis Lucy saw her in Tesco wearing two different shoes, trying to buy a 5kg bag of dried food for a cat that had died a decade ago. *She seemed strange, not herself, is she okay?* I told her to fuck off. Perhaps I am more like my mother than I like to think. Lucy let it bounce off her. She tried again when it happened. Compassion and thoughtfulness. Every word agonised over. Considered. Careful. I read every message and deleted them like I was playing whack-a-mole. I am not a good friend. I am not a good partner. I am not a good daughter. I don't let the final thought form.

JP hasn't called but there are messages. Six photos of the cat and twenty-five WhatsApps telling me how much he misses me and that he's proud of what I'm doing. That he thinks I should try to eat. Maybe some pasta pesto? Even jarred. I could add some fresh basil. That he misses me. That he misses her. That he's sorry for that last message. That actually he's not sorry. He's allowed to say that if he wants. Sometimes it's easier to type than talk. That he just wants me to listen. That he knows it's not easy. That he wants to see me soon. That he could come for a weekend. A day. That he won't come at all, that's a bad idea, this is my time. But he'll come if I like. He'll always do that. He could get in the car right now. Anton would feed Sidney.

But only if that's what I'd like. The restaurant is doing well. They did a wedding dinner. It wasn't as good as ours. Nothing ever will be. He loves me. The cat was just sick on the rug but seems fine. Too many Dreamies. A catface emoji with love heart eyes. A single x.

My thumb hovers over the screen. He has said so much. It is overwhelming. You can't explain this to anyone. They don't understand. Your husband is too perfect. Too attentive. It is suffocating sometimes. He needs to fuck up. Get things wrong. Rage. Scream. Shout. Tell me I'm being a bitch. He doesn't though. It is sometimes the worst thing in the world.

I don't know what to say in my reply. I want to tell him about the woman in the ground. I can't possibly think how to explain it to him. He will think I have gone mad. Madder. I say nothing. We are opposite ends of the spectrum. Suffocation and silence.

I call the home. The phone rings ten, twenty, thirty times. Finally a voice. Distracted and harried. Distant hubbub. It is evidently lunchtime and it is evidently chaos. I ask how my mother is doing and the phone is suddenly clunked onto the desk. More shouting. Apologies in my ear. Who was I asking about again? *Oh yes. Not one of mine. I'll have to check with her keyworker. Did you want to speak to her?*

To the keyworker?

To your mother, darlin.

And I surprise myself by saying *yes, yes please. If you wouldn't mind.* And I really mean it. I want to speak to her. I want to hear her life pulsing through the airwaves.

It takes forever to get to her.

There is shuffling and clicking and beeping and the call is transferred closer to where my mother sits plucking her fingers through the air and staring through a streaked window at the world she's forgotten about.

I hear her breath. Whistling up through her bird-boned chest. A sound like a fingerprint.

Hi Mum I say. *It's me.*

It's you she says and the words run together in a slur. But I think maybe she knows. *It's you it's you it's you. Is it? You? Lost?*

Yes I say. *Me. Not lost. Here. Me. Anna.*

Who she says and I know then and relief floods through me. I am still forgotten. She is not missing me. I relax.

I found a body I say. *Can you believe that? You always said I was good at finding things that nobody else would want. I mean it wasn't the whole body. Just a face peering through the earth, really. In the bog. Not a new body or anything. An Iron Age woman. They're digging her up now. Right now. They're finding out how she died. What happened to her. I found her. Well a man did. Two men. Or maybe a dog. But there she was. All alone in the soil. I thought she was a statue. She has eyelashes. Isn't that strange? Isn't it all so strange?*

Strange says my mother. *Strange strange strange.*

I think I know her I say. *I think I know her and I think I'm going mad.*

Mad says my mother. *Mad mad mad.*

Exactly. Mad. I'm going mad. I was already halfway there, wasn't I? Maybe more. Cuckoo. Remember, Dad used to call me that?

When we played hide-and-seek in the garden. Cuckoo, cuckoo, where are you? And now I probably am. Mad I mean. Cuckoo. Marbles scattered all over the place. And now I've found a dead body and she was probably sacrificed and the archaeologist thinks she's come back for a reason and I think she's right and I think I know her. I keep dreaming about her and I want to help her and I am stuck in the bog or trapped underwater and I can't. Mad dreams, me and a dead sacrificial tribute. Or whatever she is. However she died. It's like our thoughts are knotted. Like I can't tell when she's her and when I'm me. What she thinks, what I think. I can't stop thinking about her, about either of them. I want to bury it all. But I can't. It's driving me mad. Mad mad mad.

Sacrificed says my mother. She doesn't stumble over the word at all. Clear as a bell. I hold the phone so tight in my hand that the bones of my knuckles pop against my skin. *Can't bury it. Yes yes yes. That's what happens. That's what happens. That's what happens. That's what happens. That's what happens that's what happens that's what—*

A new voice, cool and calm. Lilting accent.

Florence is getting a bit upset. Would you like to try later, perhaps? She's fine. Just needs a bit of time to decompress.

I can hear my mother's shouts rising up around the faraway room. Shrieking. The words lost now. Just strings of panic and despair.

I hang up and stare at the wooden whorls of the beer-ringed tabletop.

That's what happens.

39

I sit in the pub and I send Lucy a picture of a pig's cock. *Corkscrew so the lady pig can't escape! Men are bastards! Love you!* She replies immediately with a photo of a flatworm and tells me they engage in penis fights. *I mean it's all a bit obvious, lads, but I actually appreciate your honesty!*

I tell JP the stain remover is in the drawer under the sink in the kitchen. He already knows that but I still can't think what else to say to him. I tell my editor that I am writing but it is not ready just yet. I'm not ready to share anything just yet. Soon though, absolutely soon. I tell her to use the headshot the agency has on file. From before. I don't want a hollow-eyed update. Thanks for asking.

I have reconnected with my whole life in five minutes flat. Lilly is still not back. I switch my phone off and order a glass of white wine. Dry. The girl blinks.

It's a liquid though.

This is a sitcom.

Just whatever you have is fine.

She gets a bottle from below the bar and unscrews the lid. I accept my lukewarm wet wine and watch the horses running as fast as they can for no reason at all.

Lilly pokes her head round the pub's door. She has a full backpack on and one of those trendy net shopping bags looped over the crook of her arm. I can see bags of crisps and cereal bars.

Did you want to get anything for tonight before we drive back she asks.

I stare at her blankly.

For the dinner? Jen said?

Oh fuck.

I drain the vinegar wine and I run into the shop and buy beers and butter and more pasta and proper cheese and two jars of pesto. There is no fresh basil.

40

By the time Lilly has broken sixteen separate road traffic laws and parked sticking out of a layby half a mile from the site, the dig has progressed. I am back in my paper suit and mask. As soon as I step back into the tent I feel something within me shift. The heat no longer bothers me. My stiff joints and the agony of waiting. Gone. I have missed her. The fragmented fractiousness that encircled me in the pub dissipates. I am back where I need to be.

The trench is dug. It is deep and wide. I can see the startling white of roots tangling with the soil. Buckets are labelled and moved out of the way.

They are beginning to pull the earth away from her. There is so much care in their movements but it is barbaric. Tools and sharp edges and rough brushes. The work is surgical and ancient. I want it to stop. I want to shout out to leave her alone. To let me talk to her.

Cuckoo, cuckoo.

Her eyes find mine. I do not look at what they are doing. I look at her. She looks at me.

I do not know how much time passes. I hold her face

with my gaze. The heat and the sweat of it all fades. She is being opened up. I am here.

Madness.

Géricault went to morgues and made art from the dead.

They clear the earth from her neck first. Reveal the curl and sinews of it. The fragile stem of it.

The atmosphere suddenly changes. Voices stop. Bodies freeze.

At first I don't see what everyone else sees. I am keeping my eyes on hers. Keeping that connection that I cannot explain and will not mention.

All around me there is a pulling in of breath. The whole tent sighs with it. It moves like electricity through the air.

And I break that beautiful gaze and I see the shape of her in the dark cold. I follow the lines of the body.

A line that falters so quickly.

The curve of her swan's neck.

Interrupted.

A darkness.

A rip.

A tear.

A cleaving.

Skin from bone.

Blood from body.

Her throat has been cut.

41

They take photographs. The inside of the tent is like lightning. Each flash makes her body glow. I want to let her fall into shadow again. I want to protect her tender flesh. I want to scream. I do scream. Softly. A whimper. The sound swims inside my mask. Nobody hears. I hope she does. I hope she knows this is not what I want for her.

They brush her with chemicals. Things that change the fabric of her skin. They put their hands to her. They touch places only the earth should feel. I am sick with it. The wound at her neck gapes. It is grotesque. Soil spills from it like blood.

Leave her alone leave her alone leave her alone leave her alone leave her alone leave me

42

It is Tom's turn to stay in the tent apparently. Keep an eye. Stand guard. Just him and the body and the night. I am envious. I wish they would all leave me alone with her. I wish I could lie down on the soft earth and tell her my story.

Instead I tell the others where the cottage is and that I will see them in two hours. They ask what to bring and I say I'm cooking something delicious but bring wine, please bring wine.

I walk back with the shopping in a borrowed backpack. The heat of the tent evaporates off me and the cold starts to wind itself around my bones. I am frozen with the fading edges of a hangover and today's wine and mud and horror. I unpack and I fail to light the fire. The timer for the heating clicks on. The radiators pulse and whirr. I should have a bath. Wash off the day. Make myself presentable for company.

I shed layers and mud through the rooms and I rub my blued flesh to try to wake up some warmth in my blood. It doesn't work. The cold is within me. I can't shake it out. I run a bath that steams my skin bright red and I pour a stream of bubbles and a slick of fancy bath oil into the water so I don't have to see the shape of my body and think about the shape of hers. Slipping beneath the surface is exquisite. Hot water slippery with oil. I unknot.

43

I fall asleep in the bath and I drown in my sleep. I am plunged into the bog water. Somewhere dark and freezing. The water holds me tight. The dirt is in my eyes. There are roots in my mouth. Worms curl through my skin. Wrap around my bones. My chest is filling with stink and rot. I can't breathe there. I can't see the sky. I am alone. I am waiting. There is something terribly wrong. I am frightened.

I see her shape moving in the ground beneath me. She uncurls her broken body. Her neck gapes and bleeds dark water. Her fingers are long and slim and beautiful. They are reaching through the greenglass wet. They pull at the damp silt. They turn the earth. She plucks apart roots and unclots mud. She does not move like the dead. She is as fluid as the bog and as solid as the earth. She dances through the soil.

She does not see me.
She is searching.
She is looking.
For something.
For someone.

I want to help her.

I want to search.

I need to find it.

I need to move.

I need to find it.

Desperation burning in my blood.

I struggle against the bind of the roots and the soil.

I cannot move.

I scream but I have no mouth

Only earth and dirt.

Searching,

plucking,

holding,

sifting,

moving,

hoping

She imagines the other place.

It is close.

It has to be

close.

She has to believe that.

But she can't feel it.

All the years of learning the turn and play of the earth.
The secrets of the soil.

Never a whisper.

It is not close enough to hear through the roots and to be carried

on the stories of the shoots that stretch

between.

But it must be close. It has to be close.
It is the only thing that

lifts the darkness.
Just for a second
                 In all the endless

                            thousands of them

44

I wake up and the bathwater is biting cold.

Night is crawling in.

They will be here soon.

I get out of the bath and my fingertips are puckered. I shiver and water scatters. I don't look down at my body. I wrap myself in one of the soft white towels that has enveloped a woman who wrote a book about dragons and a man who made a whole novel out of wanting to fuck his sister.

I can see her.

Painted on my eyelids.

Make it stop.

I lie on the floor. Press my face into the silk cold of the tiles. Close my eyes. Don't think about it and you can get up again. Don't think about it and you can get up again.

You can't stay here forever.

You have to get up.

A voice.

Far away.

Not here.

Pulled from the past.

I wonder if it is my mother.

I have forgotten the sound of her, her before.

You have to get up.

I know it is just an echo in my head.

I listen to it anyway.

It is enough. Somehow.

I sit up and the walls shift. My stomach rolls.

Food.

I have to cook.

I get dressed. Wobble as I pull on my socks. T-shirt on backwards. Struggle to understand the workings of a jumper. Head spinning again. The woman. Fingers outstretched. Searching.

Fill a glass with water. Drink it too fast. Feel it swirling in my stomach. Clenching cold. It lifts the mist a little.

My mouth tastes bitter.

Soil and spit.

45

I can cook pasta. Of course I can. I'm not Nina's useless husband Andy. Boil the water. Put the pasta in. Salt? Oil? Something like that. Flavour the water? Seems mad, you just throw it away. But when am I supposed to start cooking it all? When they get here? Or keep it warm? It is all impossible. I am useless. Should there be a salad? A starter? When my father died my mother stopped cooking. She said she hated it and it was pointless. Slaving away three times a day for something that was disappeared in an instant. I absorbed the grief of it. Cooking was for other people. Not us. Not me. Before JP I had cereal for every supper. Coco Pops on the weekend. Bran Flakes on the weekdays. The maddening sense that made to me.

JP loved dinner parties. He'd do six courses, a tasting menu, a Mexican feast, haute cuisine, Turkish brunch, Japanese fusion, Pancake Day with forty different toppings, savoury and sweet. Whatever took his fancy. Whatever he'd read about in one of the hundreds of hardback recipe books that stud our shelves. He once went all the way to Edmonton for one spice. Sometimes he'd just wake up on a Saturday when he wasn't working and he'd text all our friends. Come round, food and wine. They'd all turn up, no matter what other plans they had. Our flat would be full, fifteen people squashed round our tiny dining table. Elbows knocking. Those little orgasmic groans when the first mouthfuls went in. I would pour the wine and clear the plates and think about how astonishing the whole thing was. I read once that chefs just eat beans on toast at home or their partners do all the cooking. Too much of a busman's holiday. No interest if it's not the business of it. But it was JP's whole life. Food is love. He loved me. He fed me. He fed us all. Food shifted from something wrapped up in grief to love. And then all the way back round again.

I put the pan on to boil. I can do that bit. Check the packet. How much for six people? No, five. No Tom. I pour in the whole bag. The pan isn't big enough. The pasta clumps together. I turn up the heat. It'll work itself out.

I set the table. I've forgotten to think about pudding. There are biscuits. This is a disaster. I don't want to do it. I don't want them here. I find the red wine that came with the house. I pour some into a mug. It tastes like coffee and tannins. I am calmer. They can have the biscuits.

There is a thump on the front door and the pack strides in. They have changed their clothes but bring the smell of the bog with them. I wonder if it is in me too. Stuck deep down in my pores. Steeped inside my skin.

They bring wine and I remember the beers and no one minds that they're not cold. Martin says he actually prefers it that way and drains his in one. Some of the smell coming from him is danker and more herbal. His eyes are a little red.

Jen drinks straight from the beer bottle. She takes books from the shelves and reads the blurbs slowly and carefully. I am absurdly pleased when she pulls a face and quickly puts the dragon book back. I find more glasses and mugs and the rooms are filled with noise and it's so strange. I pass round wine and I forget about the pasta until it is cooked to mush. I add the pesto and the whole meal turns into a verdant gruel.

We sit round the table. Hugo right next to me. Lilly picks at her food. I don't blame her. I offer cheese, butter, salt, pepper. Hugo takes it all. So does Martin. The pasta isn't hot enough for the cheese to melt.

Did you know there was this bog body found in Ireland, in the 1800s? Found on farmland or something. Hugo spears a piece of pasta on his fork. It disintegrates almost instantly. He pretends not to notice. He puts it in his mouth. It is apparent he does not need to chew. *Mmm delicious. I think he was a ritual sacrifice, one to appease the gods. But anyway, the family who owned the land charged people to exhume him. Then they'd rebury him. Like a tourist attraction. Guess that was life before TV and the internet. Come and dig up our corpse! Book a slot and wait your turn! Fun for all the family! So weird, huh? Kind of enterprising though. They did it for eight years or something.*

I feel sick. The uncovering. The exhumation. The cold dark. The familiar soft earth. The tearing away of layers.

129

The bright sun on tender skin. Over and over and over again. It is too much.

I see Jen looking at me. She twists a ring around her littlest finger. A drop of golden sun.

Where is he now I ask. *What happened to him?*

He's in a museum says Hugo. He eats another mouthful of pasta and tells me again how lovely it is and I think that behind it all maybe he is truly kind. *National Museum of Ireland I think. I saw him, in the first year of my degree. Under a glass case. All twisted and flat. A bit like when you see a frog or whatever that's been run over so many times on a hot day that it's just an outline of itself. Sort of like a crispy shadow. Lovely. You can't dig a body up a thousand times and not get some sort of damage. That's why this body is so exciting. It might make my career. We're going to be able to write papers. Right, Jen?*

Jen is still looking at me. She doesn't answer.

A glass case.

All that light.

Those sacrifices, they're mad says Hugo. *They'd walk them out into the bogs, alive, because you couldn't carry someone dead across all that sinking land. They'd literally be walking towards their own death. Nowhere to run to, even if you had the energy. All that flat land. You can't hide. You know they used to drug some of them? Psychoactive stuff. Sometimes mushrooms, or even like mistletoe or whatever. Ergot poisoning was a thing. Could keep them calm, could maybe make them go absolutely mental.*

If I were walking to my death, I'd take the drugs.

And today, whoa. Seeing her like that. That wound. Right there. Like it happened yesterday. Best moment of my career. Brilliant. Definitely murder or sacrifice, right Jen? Hugo pauses with a forkful of pasta slop suspended in the air.

Murder and sacrifice are the same thing I say. I am emboldened by wine and terrible food. *What you mean is whether it was part of a cultural decision or not.*

Exactly says Hugo and eats the mouthful. I top up the wine glasses. The bottle is empty. I fetch another. It runs deep red from the neck as I pour it into mugs and glasses. *The body in Ireland, he was strangled. Something round his throat. Can't remember what. But this is much more exciting. I mean it is, isn't it? A great big neck wound versus a bit of rope or whatever.*

Mmm I say. *Probably not that exciting for her.*

Martin chokes quietly on a piece of pasta and Lilly thumps his back. I don't break Hugo's gaze. He reddens.

I mean, for us. As academics. But also, frankly, just as people. Who else gets to see this shit? It's incredible. Remember that guy with the neck wound and the caved-in head and the garrotte? Just all these marks of murder on his body. Would be so cool if we found more stuff like that as we uncover her.

This shit? Lilly is glaring, colour high in her cheeks. *Dead women? Murdered people?*

There is a string of tension taut in the air. I am suddenly sorry I started this. I don't want to listen to it. I can't listen to it. I see her. In my dream. In my mind. Moving through the earth. Searching and keening. Lost and found. This bickering, this scratching at her death, this marvelling at the wound that tore her apart. It sickens me.

I've been thinking about your book says Jen across the table to me.

I'm glad someone has. Well, actually, I'm not. I don't want to think about it. To talk about it. To discuss the minutiae of my failings around the dinner table. But somehow I am grateful to Jen for putting herself between Lilly and Hugo, for breaking the conversation open again.

You know what Stephen King says? says Hugo and I brace myself. *Stories are artefacts. Found things, like fossils in the ground. Relics. Part of an undiscovered, pre-existing world. I might have got that a bit wrong. I can always remember part of something, never the whole. It's a curse. But yeah, they exist already, stories. Writers just uncover them. Excavate them as carefully as they can. He said, he said something like there will always be breakages, losses. You can't just lift the whole thing out of the ground. But you do what you can. Polish them up. Show them to the world.*

Fucking hell man says Martin and it might be the first thing he's said since he lied about the beer. *That's deep.*

It really kind of is.

46

We sit outside on the stone steps and share a joint. Martin provides, obviously. We pass it round and I feel like a student again. I think Lilly actually is a student. She rests her head on Hugo's shoulder and closes her eyes. Their brief row has been folded away and forgotten. The dark turns sweet and clouded. The night is cold but nobody minds.

Do you think says Hugo mildly, *that there might be something to snack on? A biscuit? Crisps? Anything really. Nothing difficult, nothing that you need to cook or anything. It's not that I didn't enjoy your meal—*

I didn't says Martin. *It was fucking awful.*

Hugo swivels his head towards me. Eyes huge in the moonlight. Wide with horror.

It was delicious he begins but I hold up a hand.

Thanks for pretending. You're true gentlemen. Except you, Martin, you prick.

Martin grins and blows a cloud of smoke.

How do you even ruin pasta he asks and I mime swatting him like a fly.

It's an art I say and I go back inside to fetch some food. I lay out biscuits on a plate and they are devoured. I remember the multipack of chocolate bars and I cut them into chunks and arrange them in stupid concentric circles like I'm plating at JP's restaurant. *A smörgåsbord of Cadbury's* I offer with a little bow and everyone laughs too much and for too long.

We settle into a low hum of conversation that wraps around us. Hugo tells Lilly about the patterns of the stars. She keeps her eyes closed but she doesn't move her head from his shoulder, except when the joint reaches her. She sits up a little. Coughs. Fills the air with smoke.

The smoke curls upwards in shapes that are just so very beautiful. I want to draw them. I can't draw. I think about how I'd describe them instead. Cloudy? Twisted? Smoky?

This is what I mean says Jen and her eyes are glazed and bright. I think she might have been talking all the time I have been watching the smoke dance. *That you have the story. You unearthed her. The story is just to be discovered. You will discover it. It will come to you. All of this stress and worry, not worth it.*

I have not told Jen I am worried about the book. About anything. It must pour off me in waves. A miserable cloak of grief and ineptitude.

It will be unearthed. Trust her. Trust yourself. It will come to you she says again. Say something enough times and it sounds like truth.

Yeah exactly I mumble. *Like she comes to me. She's just not talking yet.* I start laughing. It is very funny. *Tell me the story, come on! Just tell me! Get on with it, bloody hell. Haven't got*

134

three thousand years. I suppose deadlines don't matter to the dead. *Dead. Lines. Ha!* I laugh again. Hyena-like into the starred sky. I am very funny. Nobody else is laughing.

Jen considers me for a moment. Her head tips to one side.

You found her for a reason says Jen. I didn't technically find her but I let this slide.

Mmm I say. Non-committal.

You asked me in the pub says Jen. *Why women? Why these poor murdered women? I didn't tell you then. I was still feeling you out. My feelings are generally good. I thought I knew. I was right. But sometimes it's a bit early to say. So I'll say now. These women? I was one of them. Not quite. Nearly.* Jen pulls aside the neck of her jumper and I see it.

Skin. Bubbled and puckered. Reds and yellows and whites. Crinkled and stretched.

Burned.

My husband.

I'm so sorry I say and I hate myself. It is never what I want to hear. It never helps.

Jen smiles. She twists a silver ring around her finger.

But that's why she says. *These are the women I'm drawn to. I know you might think me some foolish old woman. Looking back to the past to fix the problems of my present. But you understand, I don't have problems now. I am alive. I am lucky. So I tell their stories. I reveal their injustices. I catalogue how they died and why. I wear them on my fingers. I remember them. I do that because nobody else would. Because nobody else would know otherwise.*

135

They deserve to be known. They deserve our sympathy and horror. They deserve our anger and our fury. And why are you drawn to this woman? Only you can say. Only you can know.

She takes the joint from Hugo and inhales.

Only I can know.

I know.

47

Martin talks about how the earth is alive with death. It sounds wrong. Jarring. It's a, what do you call it, contradiction in terms. I tell him that. I don't intend to sound aggressive but I hear how my words land. Little arrows.

No it's not Martin says and he rubs his hand over his bearded face. The moustache. The strange 1920s sideburns. The sound rasps. I want him to do it again. I want to do it to him. I want to feel that wiry nest of hair against my cool skin. I don't want to have sex with him. I just want to touch another human. I want to feel a heartbeat and flesh and bones and the thrum of blood. The facts of a life. The feeling is wild and sudden.

It's not, it's a paradox. A contradiction is something that can't be true in both ways at the same time. A paradox is where it sounds like they're contradictory ideas but they actually reveal something bigger. Deeper. A deeper truth. And that's it, isn't it? Life and death. All tangled together. Both true. Both not true. Schrödinger's bogbody, if you will. That's what Jen has been saying. These bodies, the ones caught in the bog. They don't decay. They are the same structure, the same shape, the same organs. They're caught between proper life and proper death. A paradox, see. I thought you were a writer?

I should be wounded by that question but I'm not. It just makes me laugh again. The sound bounces off the sky.

So did I, Martin! So did I!

He laughs too. Throws up his hands in mock apology. Ruffles them against his face again.

Schrödinger's bogbody I say. *God you're pretentious. Should have known. Booker Prize shortlist every year? Every single year. Nobody does that.*

Martin grins. I sit on my hands. Feel the bones of my haunches punching through tendons and pressing them into the cold concrete of the step. Does concrete always feel so nice? Even through the weed-haze I am disappointed in the dullness of my own thoughts. Martin's question swirls. I can't find the laughter again. It's all escaped into the sky.

Thin places says Jen and I am reeled back into the scaffolding of the conversation that has been building around me. She blows a smoke ring into the night and passes me the joint. It is burning down to a stub. I release my left hand from under me and take it between thumb and forefinger. I hold the smoke in my lungs. Amazing how quickly you remember. Muscle memory. Hold it. Hold it. Hold it until my chest is turning to stone. Feel it burn its way into my blood. Stars everywhere. Jen's smoke ring pulling out of shape and into nothingness.

Thin places don't exist says Hugo. *It's religious nonsense.* I think my mother would probably have liked Hugo. If he didn't have an earring anyway. Lilly shifts on his shoulder. There are blue smudges under her eyes. Her lashes brush her cheeks. She looks like a doll. A bird. A tiny dreaming child.

Not a smaller gap between heaven and earth, Hugo says Jen. *Not what we're talking about here. Just life and death. In places like this they are side by side. You can touch both at once. Both held so close together. It's a contradiction, but then it's not. Another contradiction. Infinity. What did you call it, Martin? A paradox. That's what this is then, maybe. Life and death bound tight. Existing and not existing. Paper-thin gap between the two. Crossover.*

Martin is nodding. Jen taps her feet. Looks up at the sky.

Makes you think whether what we do is right she says. *Taking people out of these thin places. That poor man in Ireland. The ethics of it. The philosophy of it. The morality of it. Are we any better than those landowners, really?*

Of course we are says Hugo. He is angry. *We're doing this to understand, to link to the past, to learn. To educate. Not to line our fucking pockets.*

Definitely not to line our pockets Martin says glumly.

Ah but names on papers, names in journals says Jen. *That's not a million miles away, is it?*

Hugo is preparing for an argument. I can see the twitch of his jaw and the rush of his hazy thoughts blurring behind his reddened eyes. Lilly sits up so quickly I think she is about to be sick. But she just blinks and says in a rush *so I think it was sacrifice, right? I just have a feeling. Yeah, a feeling Hugo. They're allowed. My feeling is that it's sacrifice. Not just a single man and an axe and a grudge. It was organised. For some bonkers reason, obviously. No one was ever sacrificed for*

139

anything we'd see as sane now. I mean people are still sacrificed I guess, and it's still always insane. Honour killings. And she's a woman, right? So she'll have done something to offend the men. Upset them. Had sex with them or wouldn't have sex them or couldn't have their babies or had too many babies or the crops were dying and she was menstruating and brought a curse upon the land with her wicked womb blood.

Hugo's eyebrows twitch ever so slightly. I wonder if he's the type of man to ask his girlfriend if she could please keep her box of tampons in the cabinet and not on the shelf by the loo.

So they get their big pointy daggers or their sharpest stone axes or whatever and they open her neck and pour her blood into the earth. Bury her away from their homes, their children, their land. Punish her with this eternal life and death. Chain her to this thin place. So maybe it's all right if we take her away from that. Maybe it's the right thing. Or maybe it's the safest place she's ever known.

Jen nods.

Fucking men says Lilly savagely and then slumps back onto Hugo's shoulder and closes her eyes again. I run my eyes over the lines of her tattoos. Arrows and dots and a semicircle. Almost celestial. A planetarium inked along her skin.

Fucking men indeed says Jen.

Martin takes the last drag from the joint. Its end glows hotcoal red in the velvet black. It feels like the night is fading away from us. I want to be alone now.

I slip inside. Run cold water over my wrists. Watch the water stream and slide away from me.

Thin places.

48

She is kneeling. Back curved like a stone. Face pressed to the ground.

Screaming.

Calling.

Keening.

The sound trembles through my bones.

The howl is a question.

The earth doesn't reply.

She is suspended in the silt.

She cannot go forwards.

She cannot go backwards.

Caught.

Unravelling.

Always.

Kept still by the spill and strike of the knife

Up up up

A point in the sky

Breaking the air into pieces

Splitting life in two

Down down down

No pain

A burn
Fire and ice
Then
The blood
The blood
The blood
There is so much blood
She wants to drink it
Put the life back inside her
Start again
Start all over again

49

The blood. Excessive to the point of parodic. Camp horror. Buckets of it. Soaking and streaking and painting. The stench of iron clinging to the wind. Wave upon wave. Waterfalling. I can just see red. I am awake and I can still see blood. Taste it. Smell it. Feel the slip of it on skin.

I saw it.

I saw it all.

I saw the slice of the knife and the spurt and the rush of blood.

Deep breaths.

I didn't see it.

Cuckoo, cuckoo.

Just the weed and the wine.

Just Lilly's story worming through my mind.

Let the dream fade.

Let the blood fade.

I saw her die.

Today they will uncover her. Jen told me last night. The details appear in a dreamhaze of weed-soaked memory. Today they will pull back the final layers and let the light fall over her body. We will see all of her. She will be pulled out of the ground. Stripped from that thin place and put into the back of a van. Someone will go with her. Sit in the back with her. They'll take her to a lab somewhere and she'll be brushed and sampled and studied. Then maybe she will lie in a house of glass. Air and light where there was once only soil and darkness. Faces pressed against the panes. Her skin exposed and raw. Staring at strip lights and an unchanging plaster ceiling. Naked. Bored teenage boys on school trips, searching for her nipples, her vulva. Laughing at the audacity of it all. Taking pictures for their Instagram, Snapchatting her to their faraway friends. Showing her to the world. Pointing at the rip in her neck, the wound that fed the earth and carried her into something new. Delighting in death. Never thinking about the life. I can't bear it.

I pull the duvet over my head and push my face into the pillow. I want to stay here. I don't want to get up and watch the start of all this happening. I just want to sink into this soft nest and push away the sharp edges of the world. Become like my mother. When my father died she took to her bed for one week. It started on the day of his funeral, after the wake. My mother didn't want anyone coming back to the house. So we'd gone to some sort of function room and had funny little sandwiches and mini quiches that stuck to the paper napkins. I ate them anyway and felt sick with the richness of all those slimy eggs. I wanted to enjoy the taxi ride home. I had never been in one before. I used to see them scuttling like shining black beetles. My mother didn't believe in taxis. Not when the bus went right to our road. Today she was making an exception, and I was excited. The quiches ruined it. I had to concentrate on keeping them in my tummy. I wanted to watch the numbers on the meter. I wanted to sit on the flip-down seat. My aunt sat there instead. She rolled down the window in case I was sick.

When we got back home my mother simply climbed between the sheets still wearing her mourning black and her patent kitten heels. I remember one of them caught her tights and pulled a ladder from her knee to her ankle. She didn't notice or care. She never wore tights anyway. Too delicate to be practical. She just pulled the duvet up around her neck and closed her eyes. Flat on her back, her shoes tenting the duvet like the Wicked Witch of the East's poking out from underneath the house. I thought she had died. I was seven. I pulled at her hand. I squeezed. Tighter. Tighter. She didn't move. Her fingers were cold. Dead people were cold. I hadn't seen Daddy dead but I knew enough. Mummy was dead too.

She's just sleeping said my aunt and pulled me away to the kitchen where there were leftover wake sandwiches and some forbidden lemonade and chocolate biscuits. But sleeping meant dead, didn't it? I'd seen it on the gravestones just today. I had read them all. Children younger than me. Babies. All dead for hundreds of years. The same messages stamped into stone. Fell asleep. Born sleeping. Resting in peace. My mother never held with such metaphors but others did. That stars-in-the-sky teacher. The man who spoke about my father before the coffin slid behind the curtains to be burned to ashes. Eternal rest. My mother pursed her lips at that bit. It was religious. She hadn't wanted any mention of religion but the man was determined. He thought he could save us.

My mother stayed in bed in her funeral clothes for one week exactly. I did not see her eat or use the bathroom. She didn't speak. She didn't move. My aunt made me supper and took me to school. She read with me in the evening and tucked me into bed. I wondered if this was it now. Two dead parents. Raised by an aunt or maybe sent to boarding school. Like the stuff in storybooks. I liked the idea of a boarding school. Midnight feasts and Enid Blyton.

Then on the seventh day my mother rose like some sort of bestockinged Jesus. She stripped off the black and burned it in the fire. She made a cup of tea and asked me if I would like cereal or toast for my breakfast. I chose cereal. We never mentioned that week again.

When I couldn't get out of bed I thought of my mother. Her shoes and her black shift dress. That spider's web ladder in her tights. Flat on her back. Weighed down with grief. Sunken in the sheets. I pushed my face into the smothering embrace of a pillow and I asked JP if I was like my mother. *No my darling* he said and he curled himself around me like a comma. *You are not like a mother. You are a mother.*

But of course I wasn't.

147

50

Everyone is a little bleary and no one is complaining about the coffee. The proper catering has arrived in time for a breakfast that no one wants to eat. It is dotted along the folding tables in the white tent. Doughy half-moons of croissants and greasy reconstituted sausage rolls. Plastic tubs of neon yoghurt. Vanilla and fudge and peach melba. Memories of the clattering school dining hall.

The air is spiked with excitement. Tom is bruise-eyed with tiredness but bouncing with energy. He slept in the tent overnight. I am envious. All that time alone with her in the quiet dark. I wish I could curl up in the earth next to her. Try to hear her through the soil. Speak to her through the dirt and the roots. Tom says that he heard dinner was a lot of fun. He smirks at Martin, who is pressing his forefingers into the bridge of his nose. Martin grunts and then shakes his head from side to side like a dog. Shifting the hangover from his brain.

Paper suits are being pulled from packets. People start hopping around snapping on shoe covers. I do the same. It feels like dressing up. Pretending to be the same as them. Pretending like I have a proper job. A proper purpose.

Martin slips out with a bag of clinking tools. Tom passes me a cup of coffee.

Really sorry to miss last night he says.

What was it like here I ask.

Brilliant he says. He is so careful with his words. I am surprised when he speaks again. *Jen usually does it herself. I think she wanted to spend time with you. Sees something in you.*

I raise an eyebrow slightly. Tom shifts.

Jen is a very special person he says. He speaks slowly. Each word pondered. *She has these beliefs and these systems. Hunches. Premonitions.*

Premonitions?

She believes things happen for a reason I suppose says Tom. *Which doesn't make sense to me. How could anyone believe that after the life she's had. I don't know.*

Hugo comes into the tent before Tom can say more. He gives me a hug. He looks quite fresh. Bloody youth.

Great night last night. Just great. Good chat, great food. Nice vibes. Brilliant smörgåsbord.

I let him hug me. I can hear his heartbeat rustling his paper suit.

We're about to start he says, stepping back. He's blushing again. Two pink spots that bleed and spread across his unblemished cheeks. *It'll be quite fast today. Don't want to miss it.*

I don't want to go back in. I have to go back in. The pull of the dream. Of the line between us. I want to snap it. I want to follow it.

Onwards.

We go out into the air.

We go back into the dark.

Swallowed by the blue tent mouth.

There she is.

Burning sense of something. Relief. Hope. Pity. Love. Grief.

She looks bizarre. That poor face. That slashed neck. Poking through the ground. Out of place. Out of time.

The team starts to work. Jen instructs them. She is sharp in her precision. Measurements and positions and coordinates are called out. Movements are choreographed. Notes are taken. It is strange to see how she seems to occupy two spaces. The academic, the archaeologist. Charts and analysis. The hippy. The believer in thin places. States between life and death.

I stay out of the way. I know the steps of this dance now. I can move around the spray of soil and the shift of the buckets. I anticipate, sidestep, crouch, weave. I keep my eyes on the face. I know it like my own.

It could be my own.

I wonder if it is my own.

Staring into the blackened mirror of the past, the future, death, life. Thin places. Everything inside out, upside down, back to front. My thoughts the same. Madness. If you know it's madness does that mean it's not?

I speak to her. Let the thoughts run like ribbons through my head.

I saw you die.

I saw your death.

Why did they do it?

What are you searching for?

Hugo turns to me.

Anything she might have been buried with he says and pinches the nose of his mask and pulls it away from his face a little. *You know, jewellery, gifts, votive offerings. Unlikely if she was shunned. But we have to check. There might be something on the body. Sometimes if they're sacrificed for a cause then there were gifts laid into the ground for that purpose. We'll see. It could explain everything, or we could get nothing at all.*

More buckets. More slipheaps of mud.

The earth shifts.

It is achingly slow. It is too fast.

Then a release.

I feel it. I feel a snap, a pull, a strain. It is physical. A blow. A rip. It is within me. It is all around us, surely. The air is thick with it. They must have noticed.

The earth is being
Torn from her flesh

She is revealed.

Raw. Exposed. Light pouring onto delicate skin, hidden places, secret spaces.

Twisted brown limbs. Thin as saplings and bent to the curve of the earth. Puckered breasts. I can see the swell and circle of blackened nipples. Ribs shadowing under skin.

Well now says Jen and her voice is closer and clearer than I expected. I *wonder if that's why. Lilly. Hugo. See?*

151

I move my eyes down the struts and striations of her body.

Past the slashed neck and the hollow breasts and the place where her heart must still be.

I see it.

Oh my god oh my god oh my god.

The thread between us tightens. I can feel the hook and strain of it. It electrifies my skin. I hate it. I love it. I am insane. My mind is the sharpest it's been in months.

I knew it.

It had to be.

She sees she sees she sees

I see.

I am trapped between horror and certainty that this was always how it would be. That I have known from the very beginning. That the cord that connects us was this. We have haunted each other. This is why. It had to be this. Of course. Of course of course of course.

There is blackness creeping round me. I fight the air. I keep myself steady.

There it is.

The slump of her belly.

An airless curve.

Slack and empty.

Echoing what was once there.

What do you think Jen says. *Two weeks postpartum? Maximum?*

The blackness roars.

51

We didn't believe there was anything wrong. That anything would go wrong. We were smug and stupid. Everything before happened suddenly. Fluidly. A snap decision that somehow fitted like a jigsaw piece. We were on the Tube. We'd been to see some immersive interpretive theatre starring someone JP knew from years ago. There had been gymnastic ribbons and whale song. It was awful. I was still dazed by the boredom and pretension of it. Eyes closed. JP started tapping my arm. Gesturing towards a dark-eyed toddler carefully and seriously decorating his shoes with glittery dinosaur stickers. Giggling with delight at every T-Rex.

I want one of those he said and I said we could probably get some dinosaur stickers in Waterstones or on Amazon. I liked the stegosaurus best. *Anna* he said. *Come on now.*

Okay I said and that was that. Everything forever tipped off balance by a small boy with dinosaur stickers on the Hammersmith and City line.

It all went perfectly. I didn't for one second think it wouldn't. It wasn't arrogance. My father was dead. My mother was mad. I knew things didn't always go well. But this would. I just knew it would. And it did. Immediately.

Like we'd clicked our fingers and snap – there you go. Two crossed lines on the pregnancy test. Order received. JP's disbelief slipping into pure wild joy. *My child, our child* he said. JP with his faraway family in France. His mother reluctant to leave the country. Not even for our wedding. His father remarried a decade ago. A clutch of small boys twenty years younger than their brother. His parents weren't dead or dying but they were a mess. That was something that had always pulled us together.

We wanted to do better. We wanted to remake the past. Mould the family we didn't get to have. A mum and a dad and a baby and no one fucking anything up. Who wouldn't want that? The chance to do it properly. The chance to put it right. I was dizzy with the possibility of it.

Our child.

Two crossed lines on the pregnancy test and then a ghost on the scan. Hands waving in the darkness. Buried deep inside me. The size of a plum, according to the app JP downloaded. He always liked to link things to food. We looked at the little plum baby on the screen and marvelled at how clever we were. I didn't want to know the sex. Too early anyway. JP convinced it was a boy. *Look at that* he said, pointing.

Umbilical cord said the sonographer rolling her eyes. *Every time. Umbilical cord.*

Not even a bit of sickness. Just hunger. JP cooking everything from scratch. Of course. I just wanted forty Twixes a day. He binned a load of my processed sugar. We had a row. The cupboards refilled with chocolate. Then a foot shaping the surface of my stomach. The dome of a head. A fist. Probing the world outside the darkness. The inside pushing out. New trousers. Inexplicably, new shoes. Painting the second bedroom. Some Farrow & Ball green with a name like the worst kind of poetry. A cot. A Moses basket, although I didn't understand the difference. A pram that was actually called a *travel system* and cost more than our car. Those little sleepsuits with all the impossible buttons. Hand-me-downs from friends eager to shed the newborn days. We weren't superstitious. We bought early. Why not? We'd seen the shape of fingers. The outline of a foot. It was already in our world.

Names. JP wanting French. Me not wanting to have to find accents on my phone keyboard all the time. The cat sleeping in the cot. A birth plan (drugs drugs all the drugs please). JP wondering about hypnobirthing. Me telling him he was welcome to give it a go.

Days to go. Bags packed. Freezer stocked. Months of meals. Carefully labelled. Nina was right, a few months ago. I'd be well-fed. And JP would be a good dad. He'd read all the books. He knew how to change a nappy. He knew how many layers a baby should wear. He knew about routines and vaccines and teething and sleep cycles. I knew nothing. I'd looked on Mumsnet and found out something called controlled crying would make my baby a psychopath but also save my own sanity. I didn't read anything else after that.

Just waiting. Too big to sit comfortably at my desk and write. Another half-formed novel abandoned. I didn't care. Lying on the sofa, summer sun soaking into me. JP bringing me ice, ice creams, ice lollies. Little bowls of raspberries. Strawberries dashed with cream. Fat feet in a bowl of water. The cat lapping near my toes with his hairy tongue.

The kicking slowing down. Faltering. Unsure. Mentioning it to JP. Laziness, like their mother. I was sure of it. I was huge and slothlike. The baby had no space to turn. Trapped and waiting patiently to begin. JP was worried. Telling me to call the hospital. I did it to appease him. He was stressing about cat hair on the cot sheets, about not having enough vests, about whether the nursery was the right temperature. It was such a hot summer. He was looking at air-conditioning units on Amazon. So I did it for him. I called. The midwife told me to lie in a dark room. On your side. Drink some cold water first. Count the kicks. Call back.

One.

Two.

None.

None.

None.

Bright strip lights. A metal trolley, one wheel independently-minded. Veering. Walls rushing past. I told them I didn't need to be on a trolley. I could walk. There was no answer. Just the rush of air over my head. Cold gel. The press of the plastic probe. Silence while we waited. I knew it would come. I believed it would come. I felt silly for even being here. For wasting their time. For the rush of the journey here and the trolley and the race to the ultrasound.

Silence.

Silence.

Silence.

I was such an idiot. What a fucking fool.

The silver slip of a needle. All the drugs. More. More. Low lights. Low voices.

Waiting.

A void of time. Endless. JP crying. Me asking him to stop please, please stop. Just stop.

Stop.

Blackness.

Screaming.

Pull and push.

I don't remember.

Howling.

Blood.

I couldn't look.

JP cut the cord.

He told me she was a girl.

He told me she was perfect.

That she was beautiful.

But, of course—

she was dead.

They took her away. They weighed her. They wrapped her up in a towel. They talked to her. They laid her on my chest. It was just as if she were alive. I asked them to take her away. I wouldn't look.

JP took off his shirt and held her to his skin. I couldn't

look at them together. This is not what I wanted to see painted on my eyelids every time I went to sleep. Every time I blinked. This was not how it was supposed to look.

JP dressed her in the outfit we'd chosen. A white onesie embroidered with the Very Hungry Caterpillar. He had found it in the supermarket and brought it home proudly to show me. *Because they will be all food and books! It's perfect, non?* It felt like a cruel joke. It hit me like a physical blow. She would never read a book. She would never feel hunger. She would never feel anything. Then I was jealous. Wouldn't it be nice to be dead?

They moved us to a different room. They gave us a special cot to keep her cool. To stop her fragile tissues breaking down. Skin slipping from flesh. I hated the name. CuddleCot. Twee. Saccharine. Cutesy marketing wins again. Too far removed from the bloody animalistic horror of it all. It stopped my dead baby falling apart. It held my dead baby.

I couldn't do that.

I held her later. I wasn't going to. I lay in the bed and refused to look at her. I made another life for JP. I thought about how much morphine I would need to die.

I wasn't going to hold her.

Then I had to do it.

It was animal. I was overwhelmed with the need to push her against my skin. Try to make her a part of me again. JP laid her in my arms like she was made of glass. She was bluing. Her nails were purple shells. She was beautiful.

I held her to my chest and I willed my heartbeat into hers.

I pressed my lips into the top of her perfect head and I breathed in the scent of blood and life and death. She smelled like the earth. Something deep and dark and animal. It was wonderful. I traced the lines of her ears with my tongue. I wanted to taste her. I wanted to swallow her whole. I wanted to eat her up. Put her back inside me. Let her live forever in the dark warmth of my body. Hidden away. Protected. My blood twisting with hers. I wrapped her tiny fingers around my thumb. I held her hand. Her hands were so lovely. I told her I was sorry. She was so cold.

I couldn't understand how I would never see her again. It felt like a betrayal.

I didn't want to name her. I was sick with madness and grief and the rush and stick of blood still streaking my thighs. I thought of William Blake and his angels and his hallucinating mind writing that to name a child is to tie them to the earth. I didn't know whether that was a good thing or not. She was already dead. Should I anchor her? Should I let her go? I went round and round.

I let her go.

JP called her Genevieve.

She came back to us in a box.

The pain and the blood and the roar and the swirl of it all
The burn and the surge and the splitting of her whole self
It wasn't enough
She waited for that first cry, that first call into this strange place,
the shrieking

159

announcement of arrival and despair
that never came, never tore open his lungs with a scream against
the brightness of this new world
They took him away
Bloodstreaked and mottled
Slipped away somewhere else
But oh that face
that face
that beautiful
beautiful face
She can see it painted behind her eyelids
Never faded

52

Someone is calling my name. I can hear the lolloping two syllables of it floating like a tune. Just softly on the wind. A chirrup. Is it birdsong? I think perhaps the voice is my father's. Long-dead but that isn't a problem now is it? I mouth *Daddy Daddy*. My lips don't move.

An-na

An-na

Cu-ckoo

Cu-ckoo

The light moves behind my eyes. The blackness is sliding away now. I think I want it back. Fingers curl under my jaw. My head is tipped back. Something sparks inside me. I gasp for air. Try to pour it into my withered lungs.

Anna. Anna.

Sharper. Scared. I open my eyes. Light bursts in like a flame. Hugo above me. Just a silhouette. The glitter of his earring. Lilly's cool hands holding my head, cradling me in her lap. She strokes my cheek. Those purple fingernails. Jen is on the phone.

Her baby is dead I say and then I am swallowed into the black again.

53

The paramedics have to trudge across the marshes. Great big reflective packs on their backs and carrying a stretcher between them. I feel sorry for them. They are cheery and out of breath. Their boots are wet.

They put a plastic mask over my face. I claw at it. They tell me to keep breathing. I wish I could stop. They load me onto a stretcher. They carry me back across the bog to the solidity of the tarmac. I feel the way the ground changes beneath me. They make jokes. They ask what's going on in the tents. They have seen things like this on TV. They ask if there was a murder. *Oh that's a long time ago, not much use for us then eh?* They laugh and it is gentle and kind. I wish they would stop talking. Jen walks by my side. She catches their questions like tennis balls. I stay quiet.

I am loaded into the back of the ambulance. It is very bright. I have to keep closing my eyes. I want to keep them closed forever, I think. That would be wonderful.

We didn't go in an ambulance, before. It was quicker to drive. They even said that on the phone. Just get in the car, have you got a car? Get in the car and go now. As fast as you can. Don't worry about anything but getting here as fast as you can. We parked in the staff car park. There was nowhere else. No spaces. JP got three tickets. He wrote to the company and told them his daughter had died. They sent their sympathies and a payment deadline. It was half-off if he paid within two weeks. I suppose everyone parking in a hospital has a story like that. Nobody is special in those walls. JP paid. I didn't even know we'd got the tickets until I found their yellow skins under a pile of magazines.

My father was taken in an ambulance. I wasn't allowed to go too. I wanted to sit in the back and pretend I was a doctor. I wanted to go to the hospital and see all the needles and the blood and the operations. My mother told me to stop being ridiculous. She shouted and I shrank back. I didn't like it when my mother was angry. When I replay her voice now I find fear instead. I sat with the neighbour. She bred toy poodles. There were new puppies in her living room. Apricot and cream coloured, she said. *The most beautiful type.* They squeaked and nipped at my fingers. I played fetch and tug with them. Their tiny claws skidded across the rugs. One of them curled up and fell asleep on my lap. I had never held anything so small and sweet. I forgot about going in the ambulance and the grey look on my father's face as they loaded him inside. I wanted one of the puppies so badly I could feel the longing breaking me apart. I would call her Apricot, just like the colour of her curls. I would love her so much. I already did. My mother came home later and told me Daddy was dead now. I asked if I could have a puppy instead.

I never was very good with death.

Jen comes with me. I tell her to stay, please stay here. She calls Martin and asks him to preserve, and to wait. She will be back. She has her phone. She is with me. I am okay.

Another needle slipped into skin. The squeeze of fluids through a snaking tube. Sharp cold flooding my blood. A paramedic clipping the pinch of a monitor to my finger, the squeeze of a cuff around my arm. Asking me when I last ate. *I can't remember* I say. *I can't remember. I think it was before she was born.*

The paramedic looks at Jen. Jen doesn't say anything. She holds my hand.

The paramedic adds more clips and stickers and buttons to the body that doesn't seem to belong to me and watches the lines and beat of my life on the monitors. Green and red and blue waves. Rising and falling. All the quiet industry of the living. So much invisible effort. I wish it would stop. Let the clockwork inside me wind down to nothing.

We drive. I close my eyes. Drifting. I think they have given me something to make me drift. I want to ask for more of it but my mouth is stuck. I am stuck.

The slam of the doors and the rattle of the trolley is too much. I struggle against the belts around my waist, tying me down. I am trapped. The paramedics tell me we're nearly there. Jen keeps holding my hand. I am wheeled through the same corridors. A copy and paste of a nightmare. The swish of a curtain. It can't block the light. I close my eyes tighter. I think I am crying. I don't know if it is for me or for her.

I don't know how long I lie there. A nurse comes in every so often to check the monitors. She takes my blood. I don't flinch even as she taps my arms, struggles to find the blue lines of my veins. She ties a rubber strip around my arm and I like the burn of it. I want her to tie them everywhere. Watch me slowly fall apart. I keep my eyes closed. The drip is replaced. I keep my eyes closed. I think about how many people have died in this cubicle.

I cannot be in this place again.

I drift.

The creases of her feet

The soft petal of her skin

The tight bunch of her lips

I never got to see her eyes

I wonder what colour they were

They took him away

The man buried him without her

Of course

How could they ever let her near him now

They were already making plans

She knew that of course she knew that

She could taste the metal and threat in the air

But it didn't matter at all

All she wanted was that face

That beautiful face
Now
Soil dusted
Earthwrapped
Gone

54

I drift back. Slowly. Like pulling myself through treacle. I don't know if I want to stay where I was. I don't think I want to be anywhere at all.

Her baby is dead. My baby is dead. Those are the facts of the matter.

A doctor comes in. A smell of antiseptic and aftershave. I squint at the blue blur of his scrubs. He is young. Close my eyes again.

Ms Mendelson? Ms Mendelson? Oh okay. That's fine. You rest. Look, we've run your bloods. There's nothing of huge concern there, but I would like to talk about why you collapsed. You're really quite underweight at the moment. You're also severely dehydrated, and I don't think you've really been taking care of yourself lately, have you? Doesn't seem like you've been eating enough, drinking enough? Water I mean. Is that fair to say?

I stay quiet. My fingers touch the spikes of my hip bones. I know I am thin. I am not anorexic, seeing bloat and rolls shining back at me in the mirror. I know what I am. I do not want to be thin, thinner, thinnest. I do not want to be anything at all.

Okay. So what I think we're going to do is let you rest here for a bit. I don't think we need to admit you but I do think we need to help you out a little bit. Give you some fluids. Something called Hartmann's solution. Just to rebalance your levels a bit. A lot of women find it hard to look after themselves when they have lost a ba—

His voice is cut off. The word torn in two. Jen is a sharp murmur. I can't understand what she is saying. I think I am crying again.

Jen tells me it's okay. She tells the doctor he can go. There is some shuffling. Would he please just go. Thank you.

It's okay she says again after the draught of the curtain pulls over my face. *These women, they draw you into their stories. Into the thin place. It's beautiful and it's terrible. It's wounding. It's healing. It's okay.* She holds my hand again. I can feel the lines of her rings. Each one a dead woman. A circle of death. Never-ending.

55

I used to wear a ring.

JP and I did a register office quickie. Just us and his friend Anton and my friend Lucy. JP's mother wouldn't make the journey. Too old at sixty-five. I think she was furious that he was tying himself to an English woman. Committing to never coming home. His dad was too busy with his new sons. I took this as a sign to keep it small. I didn't have to force my mother into a wheelchair. Listen to her wail and fret all through the ceremony. It was okay. We were just keeping it small. Simple. Us.

A bunch of flowers bought outside the Overground station five minutes before. Blue and white stocks, I think. They smelled like spring and honey. We did the vows in five minutes flat. The officiant made us choose from a list. We went for option A. *Are you sure* she said. *Those are for people who can't speak English. Oui* JP said and we cried with laughter. Afterwards we had champagne on the steps of the register office and people waved from the buses. It was a London I'd never known. We went to the restaurant and the kitchen sent out everything on the menu and more. Plates kept arriving all swirled with sauces and crumbs and pearly flakes of fish and red bites of meat. Everything was salty and delicious. I ate every mouthful. There was so much joy in that food. Finally a cake, dusted with pansies. They'd made it in secret. Kept the layers frozen. They'd crystallised flowers from our window boxes back at the flat and dried some petals for us to keep and remember. Anton had stolen them when he fed Sidney one weekend when we were away. I remembered wondering why the pansies looked so bald. JP cried and I was so happy that his staff loved him. It felt important that everyone knew what I knew. That everyone loved the man I loved. The man I'd married. I'd made a perfect choice. I wore a summer dress with a lace back and I spilled champagne down the front and didn't care. I'd always laughed at the people who say their weddings were the happiest day of their lives but it probably was. When everyone had left and the restaurant was just ours JP and I danced around the tables. He turned up the music and held my hands. Pirouetting in my white trainers. Boxfresh. Adidas. I'd bought them specially. I knew I'd wear them again. I was practical in some ways, like my mother. But my mother would have been appalled, of course. She didn't hold with stilettos but women wore a respectable heel for respectable occasions. She wasn't there. I told her after. She didn't remember. She never noticed the ring. It was just a plain gold loop. Thin. I didn't want anything fancy but I didn't like all those ubiquitous stories of proposals with Haribo or gumball-machine rings. Too cute. Too try-hard. Not that there was a proposal. Just a drift towards what we both knew was inevitable and brilliant. We got the rings in Selfridges. I wanted something simple but proper. The heft of real metal. Solid and permanent. I had JP's initials engraved on the inside. My only touch of sentimentality. I had to take it off when my fingers swelled. It didn't go back on. It hadn't been on long enough for the skin to pale and indent. No ghostly trace. It's like it was never there at all.

God I miss him.

Every fibre of me aches.

56

I ask Jen if she could ring my husband. She finds the number on my phone. She tells me it will all be taken care of. She tells me to close my eyes again. She tells me she is right here.

They discharge me before JP can get here. He is coming. Of course he is coming. I do not speak to him. I am too tired. Boneheavy with exhaustion. Jen tells him to meet us at the cottage. She gives him directions, instructions, information. She is back to clinical efficiency.

They stick white plasters over the holes in my veins and they tell me to drink water, eat food, rest. They tell me not to be alone. They tell me to come back if I collapse again. They give me a leaflet for Talking Therapies I fold it into squares and drop it in a bin.

Jen calls a taxi. It is not the same taxi driver and I am too tired to be glad. I don't have any money with me. I ask Jen for her bank details. She ignores me. Opens the door for me. Guides me inside. Does my seatbelt up for me. Her ringed hands brush my stomach as she clicks the metal tongue into place. I flinch. She presses her forehead into the side of my head. Just for a second. Bone on bone.

Then she releases me, slips out of the doorway and round to her side.

We ride back to the cottage in silence. Night is starting to pull in. Jen has missed the dig. I tell her to go. She tells me to be quiet. That she trusts her team. They will do what needs to be done. She will finish it tomorrow. She holds my elbow and we cross the marshland. She is holding me up. The bog tries to pull me down. I want to let it. The porch light is on. It guides us inside. I am sure I didn't leave it on. I am not sure of anything. The door is unlocked. The key hangs useless on the hook. I haven't bothered with it in days.

On the kitchen table there is a bunch of wildflowers in a chipped jug. A box of shortbread. A multipack of chocolate bars. For a moment I think JP must be here. He would bring flowers. He loved bringing them home and scattering them around the flat. Snowdrops in the early spring. Peonies as summer bloomed. Every week and always until I told him to stop. They were the smell of the weeks after her death. Lilies. Roses. Too much. But JP would never buy shortbread. I find a small note from Tom and the team. They hope I feel better soon. It is too kind. I press my hand to my mouth.

Jen takes me into the bathroom. She helps me undress. I am too weary to be shy of the sag of my body. She runs a shallow bath as if I am a child who may drown. I sit in it with my knees drawn up to my chest. The water laps. It is not too hot. I met this woman a few days ago and I am naked. I don't care. She washes the glue of the monitors from my skin with a warm flannel. She washes silt and sweat from my hair. She brushes it carefully. Each tangle a puzzle to be unworked. Her hands are careful. Soft. Gentle. I am a body. Just a body. A relic. She treasures me. Afterwards she wraps me up in a towel. Dries my limbs. They are too heavy for me to do it myself. We do not speak. She pulls my pyjamas up my legs. Buttons the shirt for me. My fingers are not mine. Takes me to the soft dark of the bedroom. Draws the curtains before I can catch my reflection.

Bed now she says. *Just try to sleep. When you wake up JP will be here. The sun will be up. Everything will feel a little bit better. Do you want anything?*

I want my mother.

The mother before she was hollowed out by the pulling apart of mitochondria and cells, the fading sparks of synapses fraying and unravelling inside her brilliant brain, the chemistry of memories dying. The mother I never really knew. The mother who held everything together until she was pulled apart.

I have never mourned the loss of my mother. We had never connected in the way I saw mothers and daughters do all around us. Maybe I didn't try to connect with her. I was just embarrassed. She wasn't like the other mothers in the playground. I hated her for that. I began lying about parents' evenings and school plays. She still came to every single one. I would spot her on the front row with her sensible shoes and her lumpy canvas handbag and I would be furious that she had come. That she had invaded my space. I counted the ways she was different. The ways she made me prickle with defensiveness and fury and humiliation. My mother didn't wear make-up. My mother wouldn't buy me Nike trainers. My mother knitted me my school cardigans rather than buying the polyester horrors from the uniform shop. My mother didn't buy Ribena or Coco Pops or put Peperamis in my lunch box. My mother thought magazines were a waste of trees. My mother thought *EastEnders* was for idiots. I thought things would have been better if my father was alive. He had always bought Penguin bars. I missed him in a thousand ways. I resented my mother in a thousand more.

So when she first started to forget and fumble for words, let dishes drop from her shaking hands, put the teacups in the tumble dryer, I didn't reel with the horror of it. I would come home from university and pick shards of pottery from the drum and laugh. We never liked those plates anyway! I listened to her mad stories and nodded along. She became more and more difficult. It became harder to laugh. I got her the diagnosis and I backed off. I organised carers with the money she'd never spent. Drifted in and out of her life. Watched her fall further and further from the surface of her thoughts. Deeper and deeper. Darker and darker. I watched and I visited when the guilt gnawed and I signed forms and never for one single second did I think I want my mother back. I wondered whether I would like this new one more.

I want my mother.

The mother who got up and made me cereal.

The woman who sacrificed her grief for me. Packed away her mourning black and came to my plays and knitted me my cardigans and built a safe world that I couldn't wait to escape from.

I want her to come in here with her M&S plastic shopping bag and her practical trousers. I want her to tell me that this has gone on long enough. That I've had my time. That I need to face what's happened and face the world and *just bloody get on with it, Anna. Wallowing is only wallowing if you're processing. Now get up and stop this nonsense. Let's go and get a cup of tea. A cup of tea and a cry if you need one. And then onwards. Rinse and repeat. Life goes on. You can't stay stuck.*

I miss her so much.

I want my mother.

I always want impossible things.

Jen leaves the door ajar.

57

Sleep slips from my grasp. I cannot stay under. My dreams are too bright. Too real. I sit up. The moonlight is blue. It fights through the curtains. Underwater haze. Such strange light.

It shapes the shadows. They move like bodies. Haunting the corners of the room. I am not afraid. Why would I be afraid? Fear only matters if you care what happens next.

But there is something happening next.

Fragments becoming whole.

A rearranging of molecules.

The air moves. Waves of it. Light and water. I am underneath it all. I can move it through my fingers. I can make patterns with the layers of it. I can pull and twist and shape.

Oh.

Of course.

There it is.

She is here.

She is buried.

She is released.

She is here.

Of course.

She does not sit or stand. She does not hover above the floor. She just is. She exists. She is alive. She is dead. She is part of the air. Part of the light. Part of the dark. A contradiction. A paradox.

She exists.

She is here.

Of course.

She reaches for me. Her tendons move under her peat-stained skin. Her eyes meet mine. Bone white. The thread tugs.

I take her hand.

She leads me through the bedroom door. Out into the lowlit hallway. Past Jen asleep on the sofa, a book broken open on her lap. Her head lolled back against the cushions. A whistle of breath moving through this strange liquid air. She does not move. She does not know we are here.

To the front door. I open the latch. I know each next step just before it happens. The porch light still burning. Bulb throwing wobbling bars of light out into the land. It catches them and throws them back. There is nothing but darkness and stars beyond.

We step out.

Oh.

The land.

The land.

It is changed.

It is the same.

Layers upon layers upon layers.

I can see them.

New and old all at once.

A contradiction.

A paradox.

I turn back to the cottage. Its light holds it in a golden bubble but its walls are faded. Its edges flicker. It does not belong to here.

The land is low and flat. The faraway lights of the road are extinguished. The moon is bright and drowning. There are a thousand more stars above us. They ripple in the underwater air. The air that is moving all around us. Tides and waves and lines of it. A current pushing past me. Weaving beneath my feet. Streaming above my head. Pulsing.

She leads me across this new and familiar place. Along the same paths as before. Worn in different ways. Pressed flat and bursting open like petals. I do not have to walk. I am pulled along by the time and tide of it all. I move as she does.

We stop. We are not there yet. Her hand holds mine. Smooth and strong.

Walls shimmer and shake around me. They cannot stay solid. They exist only in the very corners of my eyes.

The sky is hidden.

I hear it first.

The screaming.

Bloody and raw.

Animal.

Torn in two.

Through the current I see.

A mirror of the woman next to me.

The same.

Different.

Who she was.

Who she is.

I see her.

All fours. Naked. Pulse and pressure. Wave upon wave. The air ripples with it all. The force of her body. It could pull the world apart.

A fire crackling. Smoke pulled up and swirling.

Blood and shit. Hands underneath. Waiting. I don't want to see what happens next. I know what happens next.

I have to see what happens next.

Blue. Lungs furled. Cord looped. Flower mouth. Eyelids pink and tight shut. A bud of a boy.

Dead.

Of course.

Slipped from life to

death.

Passed from hands to hands. They grasp him. Pull at his mouth. Fingers glisten in the wetdark of his throat. They listen for any gasp of breath. There is none. His limbs loll. He is liquid. He is sand. He is so lovely.

She is reaching for him. She is calling for him. Her cries pierce the waterworld around my ears. Bright and sharp. Desperate. Keening. Longing. Begging. An echo.

An echo an echo an echo.

They wrap him. They move their bodies around him. They pass him along.

A new shadow.

A man. Weighted outline. Heavy after all these women. He is expecting something. Someone.

His son.

He looks.

He holds.

He sees the blue and the blood.

He feels the stillness.

His face is fury.

He turns.

He goes.

The baby is with him.

He is taken.

He is gone.

Gone.

I want to follow. I try to walk towards the shape of his shadow. The last moment of the baby's small perfect face before he is dissolved into darkness.

Forever

I cannot move. I turn to her. She is watching her son as he slides away from her again. She has seen it a thousand, a million, a trillion times before. Every fragment is sharp and painful.

But oh so beautiful
And mine

Hers.

She cannot look away.

They took him away.

Gone.

All alone in the dark.

She cannot show me the burial. The softness of the earth as it curled around his tiny body. The songs. The prayers. The colour of the sky when it was hidden from him forever.

She doesn't know.

She didn't know.

She is haunted by it.

It would haunt you too.

58

Feet marching over soft marsh. Dark shapes cut out of swirling mist. She is by my side. She is mirrored through the rippling air. Naked. Her pupils huge and black. Dark pools hollowed in a porcelain face. Hair in ropes. Breasts swollen. Stomach sagged and curved and empty. Blood still trembling down her thighs.

She watches herself kneel. Limp as a doll. The men encircle her. I cannot hear their words. I do not want to listen to them anyway. The woman closes her eyes and then opens them again. Her head is pulled back. She stares up at the starfilled sky that she knows will be her last. Neck as pure and white as a swan's. Every tendon and bone knotted sharp against perfect skin.

The knife tears her open in a heartbeat.

Iron tang.

Her blood feeds the salted earth.

I cannot watch her die. I cannot turn away. She stands next to me. Her fingers touch her neck. The old wound dried and gaping.

They tell me
It is because I am cursed

My blood
My womb
My body
Dark with death
I will spread it like disease
I am
I must be
Returned to salted earth
To darkness
And in the dark I learned
I knew
Power and fear and fury
That was all
That was all it ever was
That
Was all it ever was

I hold her hand as her body falls.

59

Now everything under.
 All is black.

                                    Studded with roots
                                    washed by water

 It holds me. Us.
 The earth is full of longing.
 I can feel it in the grip of the soil.
 In the heartbeat of the silt.
 It moves me. It moves us.
 A rip.
 A tear.
 A fissure.
 A cleaving.
 The water and the earth and the roots and the worms.
Pulses and waves. A tide. Bearing us up.
 The release.
 The hope of it.
 Burning light.

                                              So bright

 Too bright.

The release, the relief. I wait for it. For the unbottling. Unfurling.

For the hope and the answers.

Nothing but light

But.

There is the truth of it all.

He is not here

He is gone.

Gone

Bones crumbled to dust.

perfect dust

sharing the air the roots the earth the worms the water
can that be enough
can it ever be enough

60

I am standing on the porch in the acid light. The air is sharp. I am alone.

Oh my god Anna get inside what the hell are you doing oh god Oh.

My husband.

Silhouetted. Dashing towards me. Moonlight at his back. Hands reaching for me. JP is panicking. I haven't heard JP properly panic before. It is interesting. A departure from form. Even as he drove me to the hospital he kept calm. Hands at ten and two o'clock.

He has driven through the night to me now. Of course he has. He would do anything for me and I have hated him for it. I wanted him to rage and scream, to tell me it was all my fault and that my body is poison. I wanted him to tear me apart. I want somebody to tear me apart.

I feel a rush of something. The image of the man with his knife raised. The quiet fury rolling from him as he gazed upon his dead son.

JP puts his arm around me. Presses his face into the top of my head. Pulls back. Looks me up and down. He is angry. He is afraid.

Thank god. I've been looking everywhere for you. Oh thank god. Dieu. What were you thinking? Where have you been?

Where have I been?

I look down. Follow his gaze. My feet are black.

I am turning into her.

Was I ever not her?

Cleaved.

Anna, shit, you're shaking, let's get inside, please.

The landscape has returned to my time. Lights of the road. A sky stripped of stars. Still air.

Back here again.

Anna please. It's so cold. You are so cold. Just get inside.

Jen is hovering by the door. Face pulled wild with worry. She meets JP's eye. They share a look I cannot read.

I go inside because there is nothing else I can do. I cannot go back. I do not need to go back. I know now. I knew before.

There are black footprints following me on the carpet. JP peels off my bogstained pyjamas. Goes to his holdall, unzips its mouth. Searches carefully through. I see the flash and shape of its corners before he shifts a washbag to the side and pulls out a t-shirt for me to wear. I knew he would bring it. I knew he would not be able to leave her all on her own.

The t-shirt smells like him. Salt and oil and musk. He rubs my feet with a tea towel. Rubs my arms. Sits me by the fire. Ruffles the embers, throws on more wood. The flames tongue the logs greedily. I watch them burn.

I woke up and you were gone. Jesus. Jen rubs her hands over her face. *You can't go wandering into the bog at night. It's dangerous. You could drown. Thank god JP arrived. I didn't know what to do. I didn't know what to do.* She says the last words directly to JP. He nods. Closes his eyes. A tear escapes. I watch it follow the curve of his cheek.

I understand now. Why she's been there. Reaching through the ether and the air and the soil and the bog. What she wants me to do.

Jen I say and I am calm and clear. *You have to rebury her.*

61

The funeral was just us. There were no sandwiches in a community centre afterwards. No wake in our flat where everybody ignored the closed nursery door and drank all our good wine. Just a time slot at the crematorium. Nina wanted to come. She'd leave Jonah behind. I said no. Anton wanted to come. JP said no thank you. Lucy knew better than to ask. My mother didn't know about it. I didn't tell her what had happened. Sometimes I thought I should have told her because I knew she'd forget. I could have pushed the memories into her. Buried them deep down. Stuffed her full of my grief and sadness. Left the home feeling hollow as a bird's bone. But I couldn't let her be forgotten like that by someone else.

The coffin was as small as you'd expect. People always go on about tiny coffins. She was tiny. It fitted perfectly. It wasn't remarkable. The fact she was dead was the remarkable thing. *Isn't it astounding* I said to people afterwards. *Isn't it astounding that she was alive and now she's not? Isn't that the strangest thing you've ever heard?* Before I took to bed I said it to nearly everyone I met. In the supermarket. On the bus. They didn't answer. It didn't matter. I knew I was right.

I wrote a letter and I sent it into the flames with her. I was eight years old and watching sheep bones in the fireplace. I was thirty-seven and my daughter was disappearing before my eyes. The gap between these things was nothing at all. It was forever. The letter was inelegant and sprawling. I used a fountain pen with proper ink. Thick and rich and glossy. Imagine typing up something like that. Sitting down at a laptop. Connecting to a printer. I used the nicest paper I could find. The writing was raw and rough. It was the best thing I ever wrote. It was the last thing I ever wrote.

The government paid for the cremation. I didn't know that happened. Why would I know? I had visions of some sort of municipal burning. Everybody's children sliding into the flames together. Of course it wasn't like that. The funeral director just filled in a form. He was a grey man in a dark suit and he didn't charge for anything at all. I wasn't expecting that either. It was a kindness but I couldn't be grateful that I didn't have to pay to burn my daughter or for her funeral. *How do you make any money* I said. Grief had made me bold. The man lowered his eyes. Pressed his hands together on his lap. He was good at that. The respectful body language of death. *We don't have many children.* Of course they didn't. It was mostly pensioners and the odd unlucky cancer patient or motorcyclist or people with a handful of pills and a dream of blackness. What had happened to us was extraordinary. Astounding. Remarkable. *Rare as hen's teeth.* This was presented as a sort of comfort by the midwife. *Just so uncommon.* I didn't give a fuck. It had happened. It had happened to me. I wished it had happened to anyone else at all. I wished it had happened to everyone else except for me. I didn't care about all the babies fighting their way into air and life. I cared about the fact mine was burning to ash.

Afterwards when we got our daughter back in a box, JP wanted to scatter her. Somewhere beautiful. Somewhere with meaning. *Where would that be* I asked. *Where was special to her?* I knew the answer. It was inside me. I wanted to eat the grey grit of her. I wanted every gram and molecule and cell of her to be back inside of me. I was mad with it. I couldn't tell JP. I had to put the box away. Inside my bedside table drawer. Close it up to darkness. Don't think about it. Keep a lid on it. Ha. But I knew where she was. Beside me. Right next to my head at night. I could whisper to her through the darkness.

I keep my daughter in a drawer.

I know where to find her every atom.

62

Jen does not think I am mad. I didn't think she would. JP probably does. His mad wife, shivering by the fire in a faded Bon Jovi t-shirt. Talking to a dead woman. Visitations, visions. Watching her life, her deaths, her births. Insisting she has to be returned to the earth, to the thin place, to the space that holds the echoes of her boy. That she cannot be housed under glass and light.

This isn't what he signed up for. But they listen as I spill the guts of the story. Her story. JP makes tea. I drink a little.

I told you there would be a reason you came to her in the marsh Jen says. *She came to you. Sometimes they come. When they come, we must listen. We must always listen.* Her rings throw the firelight onto the walls. *But reburial. The team.*

Lilly will agree I say immediately and I know it's true. But Hugo won't. He will be furious.

Yes Jen says. *She will.* She looks down at her rings. The stories of her women. *They gave me their stories, gave me a career. It's something I think about a lot. My role in it all. Between knowledge and respect. Where is that line? What if I have to give back now? After everything I've taken. I have given them their stories. I have remembered them. But have I given them peace? Isn't that what we all want, in the end?*

Something shifts in Jen's face. One hand reaches up. Touches the invisible ruined skin hidden beneath her jumper.

We can do it. I can do it. I will make it happen. Can you walk?

I nod.

Then we have to go now. It's my shift overnight. Martin is covering me until one. We have to go now. Tomorrow they will come and take her and it is harder to fight in the daylight.

Will this ruin everything for you I whisper. I think about Hugo. How this is one of their greatest digs, their greatest finds.

Jen doesn't answer. She is telling JP to put on boots, a jacket, a hat. He makes a thermos up. Smoky Earl Grey. Like we're going to have a picnic in the bog. He is an odd man sometimes.

I think of Jen's husband, spilling his anger onto her skin. I think of those men, killing our woman because of her body. I think of the man pulling her baby from her and taking its velvet weight to the quiet of the soil without her. I think of how JP held her. How he held me. The meat and the bones and the broth and the stock and the phone calls and my mother and the cat and the curl of his body around mine and his soft voice pulling me through the dark and out of bed and I think of the parking tickets.

I adore him.

I get dressed. Layers and layers wrapped around my trembling limbs.

Back out into the moonlight. Bright torches bleaching the stars. JP's arm around my waist. Ankles folding and twisting over the grass. I feel like I am showing off the world I know better than anywhere else. I want him to see. I want him to understand the strange fluid witchcraft of the land. He has to understand.

It is beautiful he says into the silent dark and I know then. I know.

The tents breaking the night apart. Jen tells us to wait, just wait here. She'll be back. Two minutes. She disappears. I hear her voice sliding across the marshes. Cheerful and relaxed. The murmurs of Martin's replies.

Anna JP says and I hold up my hands.

I'm not mad I say. *I mean, I am. Mad with grief. But that's all right. That's allowed. I promise you, you'll understand. Maybe not like I can. Like I do. But when you see her. You'll understand why I have to do this.*

He bites his lip.

I don't understand any of this he says. *I don't understand you. Not now. You will not talk about it, you will not look at me. You want me to blame you. Then you can be furious about that instead of what actually happened. You are stuck. I have not been able to pull you back. Maybe I have failed you. But I have tried, Jesus Christ, I have tried, Anna. You would rather have died than just talk to me. You literally would rather have died. She was my daughter too. You are not the only one in pain.*

I know I whisper. I wanted him to shout. To scream. To be angry. To rage. I didn't want him to make soup and be kind. But that was the only space I left for him.

Martin leaves the white tent and heads towards the road snaking in the distance. The shine of the Land Rover.

We hear the thump of the doors. The choke of the engine.

Please I say. *Just come and see.* This is all I can offer him now.

He gives the smallest nod. He is holding himself so very still. He is angry, I realise. He is keeping the feeling wrapped stiff around his bones. I wonder how long it has lived there. I wonder how long it has been since I looked at him.

We go in.

Jen is kneeling in front of the open grave. She looks like she's at prayer. Perhaps she is.

The body is different. It is not because of chemicals and tests and excavation. She has changed. She is ready. Skin and bone and sinew waiting to be swallowed back into the earth. She knows. She knows.

JP kneels too. He takes in the throat, the belly, the face. I watch as he sees through the layers of time and tide and he sees her. Life and death. Stillness and movement. Lost and found.

We know.

63

The buckets of useful earth have all been taken away. Off to be studied in bright white labs by people wearing latex gloves. People who will never know the feel of this soil. The touch of this wild earth. I hope they find something that is important. I hope that I haven't ruined all this for Jen. For Hugo and Tom and Lilly and Martin. For the papers they dreamed about writing. The exhibitions with their names printed smart and black on the museum walls. I have changed it all.

But this is not for me.

She will have changed. The earth will be different. There will be newness around her. We work from the spoil heaps. The mounds of dirt and mud and silt and earth have been piled up at the edges of the dig. They have been churned and mixed. A new structure. A new chemistry. All the old parts.

Jen tells us what to do. There is still a science to this art. She is practical. Clinical. Instructions and warnings. Respect and care.

I start with a spade. To and fro, to and fro. Endless. We fill the gaps around her first. Layer upon layer of black is shifted, spooned, sifted. The wound is closing. The space gets smaller. My hands blister. I can feel the raw burn of the wood on my skin. I do not care. Sweat films on us all. The air is salted with it. JP's eyes are bruised with exhaustion. He keeps lifting, tipping, turning. Spooling his anger into the earth. We do not talk. Words move between us. Unspoken on the air. I am sorry. So is he. This is a beginning. This is an end. I love you. I love you too. Shall we go on?

We go on.

Endless pouring, turning, moving, filling, working. The air is dusted. Thick. I feel the dirt clotting in my lungs. Pressing into my pores. Seaming the lines of my hands. Becoming part of me.

The space around her is filled. She is uncovered but she is held.

I put my shovel down.

It is important I do this right.

I use my hands.

I grab wild handfuls of the wet ground. I scatter it around her. On top of her. Soft and gentle. Featherlight touches. Filling the negative space. Letting the earth find its own way. Letting it cleave to her body in the way it chooses. Letting her settle into this new ground. The soil rings my blisters. I don't take a moment to enjoy the pain. It doesn't matter at all. Right now I would not choose death.

At some point I realise Jen has slipped out of the tent. It is just me and JP.

He takes handfuls too. Slowly. Gingerly. Like he is holding

a newborn rabbit, all delicate neck and limbs. Like each touch of the earth is precious.

And it is.

I bury her.

I rebury her.

We bury her.

We rebury her.

It is a repetition. An echo.

It is new. It is better.

We do it with tenderness.

We do it with care.

We do it with grief.

I watch her disappear.

I miss her.

It is the right thing to do.

I take the box from my backpack.

The box the box the box.

Here I say. *Here.*

Here in this strange thin place between life and death where the earth will hold her. Where she will be part of a thread that runs all the way through years and soil and ash and bone and flesh and bodies and life and death and rot and beauty and brilliance. Here she will be root and story and together and apart.

Here where she will never be alone.

JP takes the box. Feels the weight of her in his hands. Old ache on his face. He runs his thumb along the lines and angles that hold her all alone in tight black space. I see the shift in him as he stands in the wild wide open with her ashes in his hands.

And we take the grey stuff of fire and life and death and of our darling girl and we let her dance and fall through the air and into the soft dark.

And we sit at the graveside of our daughter and of a woman who lived thousands of years ago and we cry together.

64

We do not see Jen as we leave. I wondered if she is slipped into shadow, waiting for us to finish the story. Leaving us to our ritual. The unexpected inevitable ceremony of our loss. I wonder if she has already gone to tell the others that the dig is over. Waking them up in the middle of the night to let them know. That the van and the stretcher and the journey and the lab and the glass house will not be happening. That the papers will not be written. That the body is returned to earth. That the circle is closed.

We walk back hand in hand. I know the lines of the landscape. I do not falter. The tremble has left my bones. Release. Relief.

I cannot hear the chatter of her within me now.

Cleaved. To her. To them. To the land.

JP makes me toast in the cottage. He has brought sourdough and salted butter with him. It makes me laugh. The sound is strange and high.

I emptied the fridge at home just in case he says holding his hands up in mock defence. *I thought you might want food after the hospital.* He speaks more in hope than expectation, I know. But he will probably always hope. He is indefatigable. I have never stopped to think about it. I have never stopped to think how he never stopped. He is lining the shelves with pâté and kimchi, Saint Agur and olives, chicken soup and strawberries. He has not commented on the plastic cheese. He will mention it in a few weeks, in a few years. He will laugh about it. We will laugh about it. I hope we get that far.

JP uses the grill and not the toaster. He flips the toast with studied precision. Each side uniformly brown. He pays attention. He takes care. He would have been such a good father. It seems insane to have that thought watching a man make toast. It is still true.

I make the tea. Two mugs, two teabags. I can't remember the last time I made JP anything at all.

I bite and chew. I choke at first. I have forgotten the mechanism of food. Of eating. JP pats my back. Offers me the mug of tea. I swallow and the studs of salty butter fizz on my tongue. The crust of the toast tastes like hazelnuts. I had forgotten this too.

We sit at the kitchen table and JP holds my hand. We stink of sweat and bog and grief. We do not speak. We need to speak. I need to wrap my tongue around the feelings that have been buried for so long. But not now. I want to sit here with tea and toast and the last dregs of night and the memory of ashes sparking like diamond dust motes. There is something perfect about the goodbye. A beginning in the ending. A paradox. Perhaps.

But the dark is draining away. The sky is pinking. The

wash of the light is too much. It flares across the grime on my skin. I want to hide from it. I want to go home. I want to see my mother. New thoughts. Old thoughts.

I want to go home.

65

JP and I shower. He holds me upright in the belly of the bath. Washes the silt from my skin with infinite care. I do the same for him. Tender and slow. I treasure every line of him. I had forgotten them all.

We are bruise-eyed with tiredness but JP wants to drive back. For us to curl up in our own bed. He makes espresso and drinks four.

He unpacks the fridge again. I collect my things. They have scattered. Highlighters and notebooks and gel-padded walking socks. Mud-dried pyjamas and twists of underwear. I would like to leave them all behind. Walk out of this place naked and new.

The cleaner comes tomorrow and JP says it is too rude to leave this much mess. So I scoop it all up and repack the gym bag and the red suitcase all over again. JP carries everything across the bog to the car. I stand in the empty cottage. It's like I was never here at all. A ghost haunting the walls.

JP sticks his head around the door.

Ready?

One second I say and I take that fucking dragon book

off the shelf and shove it into the smouldering mouth of
the grate.

Ready.

66

We go to see my mother on the way back home. She is sitting in the same chair with the same jigsaw sitting untouched on the table next to her. It is like she has been frozen and waiting. She is plucking the space in front of her with her fingers. I wonder what she sees. I ask her.

I can move the air she says.

She is a poet JP says. *Like you. The soul of a poet.*

I sit next to my mother. I take her hands in mine. Let them fall slow and soft and gentle into my lap. Still now. Still. Caught in that strange thin place but I am holding her fast. She is underwater. I must hold her. This woman who folded away her grief for me. This woman who has folded herself away. I was following the same lines and creases. Smaller and smaller.

I must unfurl.

I tell her about our daughter. Her little life and death. I leave space for JP to talk. His voice carries a new story.

My mother is listening to every word.

I know I will tell her every week. I will repeat the same information and I do not care. It is not so terrible to forget. It is so wonderful to remember. I want to share her with my mother. I want to keep her story moving through the air.

67

Jen's parcel arrives a few weeks later. It has come via my literary agency, my address scribbled over theirs with black marker pen.

I should have got in touch. I should have sent a card, flowers, something for the team. My apologies. My thanks. Nothing seemed quite right. So I said nothing. I have to work on that. Always a work-in-progress.

There were news articles about the dig. Proper ones. Not just a bored local reporter. A conversation in ethics was opened up. Did Jen have the authority to do what she did? Jen's team were scrutinised. Criticised. Praised. A national debate. My part was left out. For a while I worried they would dig her up again. Disturb and disrupt them. But there has been no action. Just talk. I know that they are both slipped deep beneath the earth now. Entwined together. Sinking lower and lower. Darker and darker. They will not be uncovered. They do not want to be found.

I open the package in the kitchen. We have been to the stupid overpriced food market and I am drinking a stupid overpriced coffee and eating a stupid overpriced apricot

Danish. Food is coming back to me. Like a memory, sharpening every day. Unfolding.

JP is making a tagine. Sidney is getting slivers of lamb and mewling for more and more. He is developing a little feline beer belly, all pink and pouchy. The kitchen smells like a spice market. Our friends will come round tonight and tell JP he's a genius. I will agree. Lucy will ask me how I am and I will show her a picture of a bean weevil's penis. And then I will answer the question. I'll ask one back. I'll listen. Work-in-progress.

I strip away the layers of brown paper and Sellotape. There is only a small note in the parcel. Just a handful of words written on a stiff square of white card. Sloping script.

They didn't mind, you know. Hugo is on a burial site in Peru. A much better opportunity! Lilly is writing her dissertation on respect and reburial. She has a job offer already. Far more than I could ever pay her. Martin and Tom are with me in Copenhagen doing research. The news coverage will afford all of them more opportunities than that one dig. All is well.

Tell her story.

J.

Taped to the card is a silver ring. It is not a circle. The ends do not meet. Instead they overlap each other. Touching. Pointing in different directions. Part of the same whole.

I slip it onto the ring finger of my right hand.

Tell her story.

Okay.

68

There is old life
and new death
in this soft dark
now
stories
and soil
change
and stay
the same
moment
to
moment
the shift of water and the swell of water under sunlight
and oh
the echo of
a small hand
that small hand
in mine
holding
tight
in this moment

in all moments
the earth moves
still

ACKNOWLEDGMENTS

Writing an adult novel after so many children's books was never going to be an easy transition, but I am so grateful to everyone who helped smooth the path. Catherine Clarke, my wonderful agent, who has defined and shaped my career from the very beginning. And more broadly, everyone at FBA and in particular, Michele Topham.

Thanks to Leah Woodburn, an editor with a keen eye and a red pen wielded with the utmost sensitivity. And to everyone at Canongate – including Brodie McKenzie, Vicki Rutherford, Louise Tyler and Hannah Watson – for all of their hard work and enthusiasm. Particular thanks to Valeri, who created such an incredibly beautiful cover.

Thank you too, to my US editor Tara Parsons and everyone at HarperVia.

Thanks so much for archaeologist Hugh Nianias for talking me through the details of a dig and the history and ethics of bog bodies. Any errors are mine, or have been included for the sake of story.

I am indebted to my usual gang of author friends – Ross Montgomery for working through the original idea with me, reading endless mangled scenes and always making the right suggestions. Jenny Pearson, Struan Murray and Phil Earle for reading drafts and stroking my ego when I needed it most.

Thanks to Ben Burton for explaining poetry to me patiently and thoughtfully – for about the last 15 years. One day I'll get there.

Thanks to Malcolm Balen and Karen Meager for being the very best parents I could hope to have, and for supporting me through every endeavour.

And finally, to Patrick. Thank you for being everything, always.